Aphelion Sky:
Ex0dus
A Novel

PHIANNA REKAB

Aphelion Sky: Exodus
A Novel

Phianna Rekab

Published by Greenstone Publishing LLC
1st edition

Aphelion Sky is a work of fiction. Names, characters, places, and incidents either are the product of the author's imagination or are used fictitiously. Any resemblance to actual persons, living or dead, business establishments, organizations, events, or locales is entirely coincidental.

ISBN: 978-1-7328807-4-0

DEDICATION

For Bariq

PEOPLE & PLACES

- Humans: 90% or more organic

- Cyborgs: a machine with human origins augmented with more than 10% cybernetic components

- Com-Borg: a self-learning companion machine that is 100% cybernetic components that can be customized to a human likeness and has no learning and evolving boundaries

- CB-V / CB-X: the first and second generation of Com-Borgs

- Borg: short for a cybernetic machine. A cyborg or Com-Borg.

- Dargav: an amorphous civilization in the Trillium galaxy

- Vyotrian: A Dargavian sect with secretive timekeeping knowledge

- Trillium: A galaxy 6 trillion light years from earth

- Atomics: Super intelligent amorphous beings who reside beyond earth's galaxy

i

ACKNOWLEDGMENTS

You. Thank you for reading. I care how technology impacts our world. Let's shape it together.

Maybe there's some truth in fiction.

"Time is the most precious resource we all have." – Steve Jobs

PROLOGUE

Time.

Time is the omnipresent, unbiased, unstoppable overseer of life on earth.

Time has no fealty to anyone or anything.

Time is the master that keeps watch, the constant guardian ensuring man is kept on track and in check.

Time tells where man must be, for how long and when it's time to move on.

No one gets to ignore or overpower Time, except for Space.

PART 1 - TIME

1 CB-V

Light from the long hall shifts momentarily to dark before glowing bright again. In the distance, like an exploding bullet, a door slam. I reach for the doorknob. It turns halfway then stops. Locked. My chest burns trying to catch air. The next room only a few feet away gives me hope even though the familiar hum gets louder.

Warmth trickles down my forehead to my cheeks. My hand grabs the doorknob and turn but it slips. A bright red covers my palms, arms, top. Another door nearby slams shaking the walls like a mild tremor. I wipe my hand on my thigh and grip the handle twisting left and right. It barely turns and remains shut. Shit. I eye the door to the last suite. I run to it, twist the handle. Locked. My rolled fist pound the wooden exterior but I know these rooms are all empty. The machine's vibration rattles my bones. With nowhere else to run this suite is all I have. A swift kick to the door but it heaves and stays shut. I launch another, and another closer to the handle. The sound of cracking wood and a quick duck from the projectile is a small victory.

The door swings wildly smashing up against the wall revealing a spacious and dark interior with executive furniture. There's nowhere left to run. I'm eager to enter for the safety, if only temporary. Regret fills me not having a way to bolt the broken door. Behind me its shadow lurks, flicking in and out, reflecting off the bare walls. I retreat further towards the back, running my hand against the wall praying for an indentation that'll tell me the suite has an adjoining room.

Three walls of solid black box me in. A tall silhouette fills the doorframe blotting out the only light coming from the hall. I hold my breath waiting for it.

Two red LEDs scan the room bathing me in a translucent red. Marked. The thunderous weight of its body splinters the floor beneath its feet as it charges at full speed. A shoved chair in its path buys me a second to dash to the room's opposite side. Its head turns mechanically towards me, eyes glower. With one hand it lifts the chair and flings it across the room. It lodges in the middle of the wall. Taking a step forward, red glaring eyes tears through me with searing heat. I step back. Long metal arms lurch but grabs air. I double back. The light is my salvation. Flying, falling, crashing my body lands face first on the shattered hard tiled floor. *Get up.* The ComBorg takes another step towards me. I'm trapped.

"Shelly."

The machine-smoothed voice violates my ear. There was a time, one day in particular when I couldn't wait to hear what its voice sounded like. Now it's the same as fingernails grinding against a chalkboard.

"Stop this right now, Kirk.   Terminate your program."

"I can't do that, Shelly."

Its innocuous voice is level, calm. Too calm for this situation.

"Can't or won't?   What you're doing is wrong. You're causing harm to a human."

"You're incapable of knowing what's best."

Slowly I dislodge my trapped feet from the crevice in the floor. Life returns to the rest of my body. My pounding heart deafens the increasing incessant hum emanating from it as it nears. I'd rather die than see its face again. The doorway is clear. I get to my knees and make a run for it.

Like a ghost Kirk appears, blocking my escape. It lets out a piercing shriek as its body rumbles releasing a multitude of holographic spawns to fill the confines of the room. They edge closer, closing in and around me. After all this time running, I'm finally caught.   A glimmer of light catches my eye filling me with new energy. The doorway is still my ticket out. My one shot. Rising to my feet with eyes fixated on the light and overpowering darkness in my way, I slam my shoulder into its cold steel body.

I wait for the crash, the pain, the victory.

Nothing.

More tricks. New tricks, but I'm through the jamb tumbling, hurling uncontrollably into the light as the ground gives way. Xavier appears before me. I reach for him but he fades into the dark as I'm pulled forcibly through the silent, cold and narrow depths of empty space. With nothing to hold, to grab, deeper, further, faster, I freefall in a pit of endless black.

"Shelly!"

I can't stop myself from falling. A powerful force from nowhere grabs hold of my back, pulls me in with a suction. There's no fight left.

"Shelly."

Bright white light floods my vision.   Brown-grey eyes, a stubbly cheek with hints of pre-mature gray, pink tinged lips, sun burnt complexion and a yummy lemony musk. Hmm.

The fear in my heart is flooded and chased away seeing him but it races, aching from the scenes before. Dressed in a white t-shirt and dark boxers his lean frame is nothing short of angelic as he peers over me.

"You just had another, didn't you?"

His voice is calm with a hint of worry and accusation. No good morning, hi honey. He pries the crumpled white sheets from my hand. They're undeniable evidence.

It was the first nightmare in a while. Okay, a week.

"It doesn't matter."

I'm suddenly ravenous and reach for his hand.

"Does IxTar know?"

"Babe, do we have to do this?"

I pull him closer, play with his fingers.

"Why won't you tell them about these damn nightmares?"

He looks me squarely with a seriousness I know too well. It upsets me when anything upsets him but this isn't the way to start a new day. My body slowly cools as dominant emotions only he triggers switch to my everyday self.

"You think they'd let me sit on their most influential board if they knew I was still working through the incident? They think it's over, done. Why rock the boat? Let it be."

I wait for it, his usual suggestion to remove my cranial mesh on the black market so the powers be would never know. I've seen the sad results of some humans who went that route.

I kick off the sheets and run to the ensuite, closing the door behind me.

The fresh scenes from the dream slams me in the dark.

"Lights on. Shower on. 100 degrees."

The steaming water beats against the tiled floor and the air is filled with spearmint and eucalyptus. Deeply I breathe in the relaxing scent. I look in the mirror. It quickly fogs, then clears. My cheeks are puffy. Curious eyes travel further down my body and stops. *How could he choose serious talk over this?*

"Temperature 100 degrees."

"Maintain."

"Maintaining 100 degrees."

The lull of the water and the quieted computer brings on the dream flashback I know not to fight for it only makes it worse. I allow it to run its frightful course.

It was just a dream. Just a dream. But it felt real. So real.

I peel off the flimsy t-shirt and jump in the shower.

"Hurry up in there. I'm making you breakfast."

His voice pierces my fear and worry causing a reflexive smile to cross my lips. He's so bossy. But I love it.

2 SOFTWARE

"I t's just software. It's either updated when the newer version comes out or completely replaced with one that has better features."

Easy for him to say. A misnomer if I'd ever heard one for lines of computer code written with the intent to do one or more things exceedingly well that may or may not be good. Hidden between the lines are the spyware instructions no one ever think about except the programmer and the ones using the outputted data. Shameware surveils what humans and cyborgs do and publicly shame them to force better behavior. Friendware anticipate needs and convincingly push suspected or confirmed interests to unaware consumers. Lifeware alerts or quietly steer the public from dangerous or possibly dangerous situations without causing widespread panic. Yes, Xavier. It's just software, but sometimes it's much more than that.

Xavier has been my touchstone for the three years since the incident. Even though we try to forget about it I know I won't. Maybe I can't.

When anyone in my circle talks about Kirk or the events that followed after I brought him into my life, they know to refer to it simply by two words—the incident. It says it all.

The implanted quantum cranial mesh wards off the worst of the recurring nightmares and help me function during the day, sensing whenever memories of Ian come to mind, softening the gut punches thrown by an increasingly apathetical world and the realization I'm spending hours in an environment where new machines like Kirk are being made. A calming dose of a dopamine inhibitor sets me right but it's like cheating at life, chemically subduing the one thing that makes me uniquely human—to feel. No one knows it's there, this little wonder of a cybernetic component is the most augmented a human can get and retain their humanness. Maybe it's practice for what comes next.

My Pulsometer beeps. I know why. Just can't bring myself to delete the message I received a month ago. Opening it will only confirm my fears I'm one of the many victims of the massive data breach that had occurred. Dr. Armsby's patients out themselves with their public uproar over their loss of privacy and the degradation of trust. After paying a premium to avoid the free public health services in exchange for security and discretion, so sensitive medical matters are kept secret, their information is blowing in the wind. Their vocalized displeasure only confirms their identity, adding yet another datapoint for those whose job it is to collect information.

Dr. Armsby's apology has done nothing to stop what has come next—the targeted Lifeware notification from the Public Health Advisory Council, the national health magistrate who demands all of Dr. Armsby's patient's records in the interest of protecting the public welfare.   The encrypted notification sits ominously on my Pulsometer with fancy words telling me I'm screwed. A recent upgrade intended for cyborgs was erroneously pushed out to humans with a cranial mesh.   The device will malfunction rendering the cerebrum irreparable damaged if the device is not removed immediately.

The PHAC would never use the words brain dead, for they had a solution for that—full augmentation— the final stop on the augmentation spectrum, but that's what it is.

Augmentation is the number one reason for a quickly declining human population that's forbidden to procreate naturally for the number two reason— having an offspring with a tainted gene threatens the viability of the cost-free public health system. In earlier affordable healthcare programs, the small number of unhealthiest humans accounted for approximately thirty percent of all healthcare costs making premiums barely affordable for the healthy majority who had no choice but to comply, as the penalty for going without coverage was quite high.   To control medical costs, a couple's perfect genes are selected or the imperfect ones corrected to design their offspring in a controlled and monitored setting.   Shameware made it easy for compliance.

The transition to cybernetics and having components programmed to outperform their organic counterpart is the holy grail of twenty-first century medicine. Be it an arm, leg, eye or a failing organ, a cybernetic equivalent ensures longevity and minimal costs to maintain. The augmentation doesn't need to be driven by need; a want is equally provocative with the government gladly footing the bill. Their wildly successful campaign changed public outlook from being a stigma to being an admirable trait. To sweeten the deal, augmenters receive free healthcare and a monthly universal basic income under a program dubbed the UBI+HP. In exchange, augmenters freely allow all their personal and private data to be harvested for any purpose. They are called cyborgs.

The ones opposed to augmentation are called Outliers. They do everything in their power to hold onto their humanness by staying off grid and refusing the government's UBI+HP offer. They use the black market for anything they need including medical care to guarantee their privacy and live way below the poverty line and mostly out of sight from public view to protect their identity.

And then there are the humans like me who fall somewhere in between the extremes of the two. Privacy is highly valued but we know in some cases it's a worthy sacrifice to live an okay life. We make the careful calculation to determine what information we want collected and shared, find ways to navigate the system being aware medical information is the most prized.

Maybe it's working alongside robots, cyborgs and automata—our partners, assistants and service providers that rubs salt in my wounds. They're the desirables, the perfect ones who've made being a human a novelty. Our frailness is a reminder of how far they've come in a short while. I miss the days when a good morning, hello, howdy was really meant and not just a warning they're about to ask you for something.

Cyborgs push to make themselves better, giving up more of their human frailness in exchange for the latest cybernetic augmentation. They recursively make machines and cybernetic components better, faster, smarter, smaller through sophisticated software and reap immense cost efficiencies. They're programmed to be that way. Never satisfied. Never letting well enough alone. In their eyes there's always better. In their eyes choosing to remain a human is an admission of weakness. No wonder Kirk overran the boundaries of his program. Better is good, if you're one of them.

For those who'd benefit from a machine as a companion to give them a boost in competing in a world more populated and dominated by cyborgs, there's the ComBorg and machines like it. A ComBorg is a 100% cybernetically enhanced programmed machine that has a human-like body and is capable of exponential learning. They're more than mere robots. They're the quintessential evolution of the cellphone from decades ago with the option to add various specialized modules for increased intelligence and capability. I wanted a personal assistant to help manage my day-to-day. The ComBorg seemed the perfect choice at the time.

No one would have thought the words brave or courageous would be necessary in regards to owning a piece of machinery. Was anyone thought brave or courageous to own a cellphone way back when? But now we know—when new technology is implemented without being properly vetted and without an oversight board to ensure safety, stuff happens. Bad stuff.

The road to augmentation and becoming a cyborg is a slippery one. Some humans start off small, getting a cranial mesh, a device installed below the skull that has a built-in computer to detect when a natural neurochemical is spiking or dropping and administer a micro dose of a synthetically created one to bring them back to equilibrium. You know the kind of emotion spike a teenager might endure seeing their first love (Ian) closely intertwined in the arms of another or being chased by a crazed machine (Kirk) hellbent on making you happy according to its skewed definition of happy? Yeah. Some humans are lucky to have good coping skills and bounce back from traumatic events like they're nothing but there are some who are naturally hypersensitive who feel a little bit more especially when they also have issues with attachment. The cranial mesh was a miracle that helped me to get over Ian and meet the love of my life. I'm still a human.

My body has less than 10% cybernetics. Anything above 10% categorizes the individual as cyborg. All it takes is one more cybernetic augmentation and I'd lose my human card. The peer pressure is strong, hard to resist, if only for the prestige and desirable fringe benefits the state and government push nonstop. But remaining human is the new virginity. Remaining undefiled is my greatest wish, the thing many humans like me fight for every day.

Better features. Xavier's words echo in my mind. Would he think a cyborg has better features to want to cuddle with it every night? If I gave in, would he still trust it's me, just a little colder? Would he still want me?

Sometimes he lies in bed and watch as I thrash through my dreams. Running away from the IxTar ComBorgs and the cyborgs on the Genesis. The vivid scenes replay like it's imprinted on my brain. You'd think I would know by now not to go in the last suite. He thinks with each dream I'll find a way to overcome it if I can remember to grow some balls, face the dangers instead of running. No luck there.

"That's the only way the nightmares will end."

I believe him. That's why I work for IxTar. They're the creators of the ComBorg—the first generation of the machine that tormented me. As a product consultant with oversight, I have input into how the next generation of ComBorgs are built. I review fail-safes and evaluate them on the basis of whether it would have helped me if they were in place when I needed them.   Besides that, our machine language experts need to be closely evaluated by a bonafide human trusted with oversight to ensure there's no bias in their treatment, unfairness in performance evaluations when compared to cyborgs. They're imperfect like most living organisms with needs to survive and learnt biases that can be transmitted like a virus.   They're the ones programming IxTar's ComBorgs, teaching them how to think and interpret our world to make decisions for us.   We look for behavioral cues to tell if their worst qualities are being built into the algorithms and computer programs but we too are imperfect and could miss something vital.

A coldness covers me. I would never consent to becoming a cyborg, partial or full. How could I still be me with flesh replaced by the most durable plastic and impervious titanium? IxTar would have no use for me as cyborgs are a dime a dozen. Xavier would never go for that in his heart or his bed. I'd be, essentially dead.

3 CB-X

The ComBorg X, the latest unreleased version is coming today. Other important things linger on my mind but there's no one better to test the machine out before it's deployed for mass consumption.

Consumption—machines consume nothing but energy, steel, plastic and data. Humans consume an abundance of food and goods made by mindless and tireless machines. For humans to survive they must find a way to become stronger, smarter and empowered. A ComBorg companion is one way without irreversible augmentation, but they must work properly.

The last thing I want is for my new ComBorg to have any likeness to Kirk. That was my one requirement when they asked me to choose a persona. Everything else they decided would be a surprise.

My stomach churns seeing the clock move to 9:45. They'll be on time as that's their service hallmark. I haven't gotten the nerves to tell Xavier about the PHAC's notification. We wouldn't be casually taking delivery of a ComBorg if he knew.

"Babe, you don't have to do this."

His arms wrap around my waist as I put the last dish away and pull the plug from the sink to let the soapy water out. The glint from the sun peaks through the window blinds. Sunrays waltz with swirling dust particles when a drone swarm flies by overhead on their peacekeeping mission. They hover just below the clouds like blackbirds in formation causing the sunlight to flicker. The streets are empty otherwise. At one time, it would be dotted with Kiley, Morty, Henley and Amit riding their bikes up and down, attempting some do-not-try-at-home stunt they saw on holovision. Now, even the trees hardly move.

"I told them I would. I vowed to never let another machine get out of control like the CB-V. It's my job and the only way I can truly move on."

His strong but gentle arm turns me around to face him.

"It's just software. There's nothing wrong with the machinery. It's what goes into it. If it malfunctions, slip out the old and slip in the new."

"I know."

"Then why are you so nervous? You've been up since before dawn and have cleaned the entire place twice."

How can I be objective with my assessment of a ComBorg when I'm battling my own impending life crisis and fears? What if the programmers made things worse or we missed something important—loosened a control gate making it possible to be breached or a weak robot law with a dubious clause a smarter machine exploit? Humans who placed their trust in the machine could be manipulated, further weakened adding to what seems an impending extinction. We don't know what we don't know. Maybe I'm not ready to be used as a guinea pig again. Maybe I should focus on myself, let IxTar work out their own issues. This is a mistake.

The pink and blue of a dwarf hydrangea pops against the browning lawn. Bees sniff at the flower while squirrels chase each other up a nearby tree.

"Do you ever wonder if this is heaven?"

"Babe, you know how I feel about that kind of talk. If this is heaven, what does it say about us?"

"We tried to improve upon something perfect and broke it."

"'Perfect'? That's an interesting word choice for a techie. At what point in human existence was the world perfect? This is the future your parents could only dream of and their parents too. I mean, you'd give up your Pulsometer, our microwave, the autopilot feature to live a more simplified life? Ms. Always running late find time to boil water on a wood stove to take her hot bath? You're just being sentimental."

"People only see the outside of the package and think, ooh, it looks nice. But behind the casing, what's in the code? What are we not seeing? And the speed at which contamination can take place and how stealthily bad code can be hidden is worrisome. You know the code we wrote for Kirk was flawless, not one programmatic bug. And how it was trained to think and interpret our world worked well in our controlled environment. We were so sure this machine was safe so we let an impressionable machine loose in the world not caring it would be exposed to contradictories, bad behavior, competing morals and supposedly good intentions. But how else would we know it wasn't ready for the real world but to set it loose and see what happened? If the programmers knew what to look for, they would have found it but you have to know and they didn't know until they saw it. We didn't know and we screwed up. IxTar made it and saw it was good and that it did good and unleashed it to do as much good as it could and that's precisely what it did, only to me it was bad and unwelcomed. 'The road to hell is paved with good intentions.'"

"It's not like programmers' thoughts and behaviors can be peeled back so their undignified layers and questionable beliefs are exposed."

"But even so, who would judge, formulate the questions, administer the test? We're all tainted with our own quirky beliefs. Nobody is all wholesome and completely upstanding. Even the best of us knowingly and unknowingly contribute to systemic biases we want others to accept as normal. I mean, most people think they're good and well-intentioned, right?"

"Yeah. Unfortunately, trial and error are all we've got. We better have a way to set things right again if things go south otherwise the setback will crush us. It would take months, years to rebuild trust. But, babe, IxTar has some of the best in the field, and they've got you. With you on that IxTar board overseeing this new CB-X I bet this model will exceed all the hype and have all the necessary fail-safes in place. That, by the way, proves my point."

He kisses my forehead like an exclamation point and holds me tighter. We rock gently to some soft music playing quietly in the background. I repeat Xavier's now famous phrase willing myself to believe it.

Slip out the old and slip in the new.

"IxTar does have some serious competition with HalBorg though. For once I'd like to see the old goat lose."

Xavier jealous of someone? That's new.

The AI-based personal assistant market has grown with two new competitors producing their own models. HalBorg Industries is IxTar's fiercest competitor. The CEO is a flamboyant megalomaniac, still a genius, whose business model is slightly different. He sells base templates of artificial intelligent personas to customers for them to build-out their own likeness in the comfort of their homes. They are digitized without an exoskeleton for ease in distribution and mobility. He believes every human and cyborg should have their own alter ego in the form of a souped-up digital holographic representation of themselves to help humans compete against cyborgs and other machines so they live better lives. yAI—you as AI—is the conqueror of deep fakes and the first entrants in the Human as a Software market. What could be more real than a deep emulation of one's self they personally train? It's them, but their replicated better version. Faster, smarter, stronger, flexible and mobile. IxTar's ComBorg on the other hand is embodied, made of plastic and steel. It's an assistant that's a friend and trusted, reliable partner. That's the intention and how it's advertised.

Halborg's business is quickly growing, selling to anyone without a background check unlike IxTar who sees it as social responsibility. The ComBorg is selectively marketed to people matching a demographic to control saturation and devaluation. Customers eagerly fill out applications and join the lengthy wait list hoping they'll be selected to get the next model. The last of the bugs are being worked out, thanks to yours personally. IxTar knows their reputation is on the line and as a technology leader their processes are industry standard. It took a lot to get here, including a Congressional hearing after the incident.

A sound outside disturbs the tranquility. I pull from his arms and head to the front door. My stomach flips, rises to my throat and I'm tempted to rush to the powder room. The large black truck with the popular manufacturer logo on the front and the letters IxTar in bold splayed on the sides, pulls up alongside my driveway. A loud beeping sound fills the quiet of the suburban neighborhood as it backs up and adjust its wheels to park close to the curb. I open the door and take a few steps to get a better look. Xavier follows behind but remains inside.

4 DEJA VU

A car I'm sure I've seen before parks in front of the truck. The driver's faceshield slides down to cover her nose and mouth. Finally, she exits the vehicle and heads towards me. I take a few more steps to meet her halfway along the driveway. Xavier inches to stand in the doorway.

"It's been a while."

I can't remember her name, Bernadette, or something similar. She's the one who had delivered Kirk and I guess she's good at her job for here she is still driving her gas guzzler.

"Three years. How've you been?"

I match her rolled right fist, lifting my arm before letting it drop to my side.

"Just peachy. So, you're upgrading."

"Sure am."

"Good for you. What happened to you was just awful, by the way. I'm glad they've got it figured out this time with the CB-X and you'll have a better experience."

"I certainly hope so."

"The meet team is here. Your programmer is Bari and the driver is Teddy. Well, ready or not, the first ever CB-X is here. Go meet your new assistant."

I walk towards the truck with every step telling myself I can do this.

The middle panels slide open like elevator doors until they're folded to the sides. A huge Styrofoam case with the colorful image of a friendly Com-Borg interacting with a happy family in their home is plastered on the casing.

The stairs slowly extend from the truck's edge until it meets the driveway.

"You've done this before. Step on up and get him powered."

Burnt rubber smell is so overpowering it makes me nauseas. I jump when the battery-powered hum from the truck stops abruptly. From the corner of my eye, Xavier steps away from the front entrance and head towards the driveway. He pauses in an attempt to keep his distance like I've given birth and need space to bond with the machine.

On one side of the case are several plastic latches to unhook the Styrofoam. I unsnap each one. The unit is exposed. Its face is covered by a plastic layer to be peeled off. My heart pounds and my fingers shake a little reaching for the plastic tab. *I'm ready for this.*

I pull the clingy layer off. His dark tan is like black coffee with a hint of cream. Chiseled masculine features emerge with thick lashes stemming off closed eyelids. Its physique is perfection, or at least perfect for a human male, six-feet tall, one hundred eighty pounds. Nose and lips are non-binary. I continue peeling the plastic tab until it hangs loose in my hand exposing the machine that's completely dressed in black scuba type short sleeve shirt and full-length pants, taut against the thighs. I drop the plastic and catch a glimpse of its bare feet.   They come that way to adjust to the new environment, learn the stairs and contours in and around my home. I reach around to the back of its neck, locate the little power button and firmly press. A haptic vibration let me know the unit is booting up. I step back so the first person it sees is me.

The eyes flick open, blue and vivid.   It smiles widely. I can't tear my eyes away seeing the new machine reveal itself as Tom.   I wonder how much IxTar paid to be able to use a celebrity's likeness and who else they managed to convince to add their persona to their portfolio.

"Shelly."

"Um, hi."

"Call me Tom. Is that suitable?"

"That's original."

I'm not sure if the voice is Tom's, but it's masculine, gentle and warm.

"Shall we go inside?"

I hold its arm as it takes its first step out of the encasement and then down the three steps onto the driveway.

"It's a lovely day."

The conversation is fluid and not as robotic as Kirk, when he was here.

Bernadette and Bari watch us from the side as we walk towards Xavier and the entrance to my home.

"Xavier Vinson."

Tom abruptly pause as he passes Xavier. He takes a step back and turns to face him.

"Penal code 5568. You've failed to pay your traffic violations. You're a derelict, Mr. Vinson."

Xavier is motionless. His eyes fix glaringly at Tom. Muscles in his jaws, teeth and fists are clenched. Everyone appears frozen not sure what just happened.

Bari springs to life and rush towards Tom.

"Ms. Greene, I'm so sorry. It's an Easter egg. I'll remove it."

A little later we're going to talk how this machine interjects in people's lives, the invasiveness of biometrics and carelessness of some programmers. We watch silently as he removes a panel on Tom's back, connect a handheld device and type frantically.

"All done. I'll make sure my team uploads the code change to the repository. Don't want this going rampant."

"Thanks.   Maybe not introduce additional complexities to an already complex program, especially one in Beta?"

"I apologize, Ms. Greene. It won't happen again."

Tom reboots and comes on-line. After a brief pause surveying the environment, he looks at me and smiles. I lead the way and he follow me inside.

"How lovely it is in here. Would you excuse me while I make myself at home?"

"Of course," I said, still following closely as it makes its way around, syncing with the appliances and my Pulsometer.

"All is well on this level. I detect my charging station in one of the upper rooms."

It heads towards the foyer and make its way up the stairs.   Every movement appears so life-like.   It's difficult to imagine the technology has evolved so much. I allow it to go upstairs unaccompanied to build trust, for both of us, though there's lingering burn pains from the little incident courtesy of the first version.

Xavier keeps his distance but watches the rest of our meet unfold.

"Does that machine know to only scan and sync with *your* things?"

His voice has traces of resentment as he stresses the word 'your'. Tom drew blood before stepping foot in the house calling out Xavier's traffic indiscretions. The thought hadn't occurred to me though. Things had changed since Kirk. Xavier and I now live together so I had him to consider in most, if not all decisions. Funny how trauma makes you see things different. Ian was so yesterday and I couldn't continue to shut out a man I adored and one who welcomed me into his world. Best decision ever.

His motion catches the corner of my eye as he walks away without waiting for an answer. He brings up a hologram of the sports schedule and sinks lazily into his favorite chair. I search his face for a hint of what he's truly feeling but he's captured by a call in the game he selects. The shouting will begin any minute as he walks courtside in the simulated stadium which will thaw the frostiness he sports which is a departure from his usual cool and playfulness. He waves to some of his friends watching at home who too were lucky to score virtual courtside seats.

"Hey, babe, it's Habib and Alek. Can they...?"

"Not tonight, hon. Tom, remember?"

I glance upstairs.

"Little fucker," he says under his breath.

"Saturday? Sunday?" I say, to lighten the mood.

"Make it Saturday. We're heading up to Santa Fe on Sunday, after the HalBorg shindig."

"That's tomorrow."

"Shit. Maybe we should cancel."

Xavier is friendly with all the heavy rollers in the Silicon Valley AI market. There's always something going on where one of them shows off their wealth and recent advances in the field to their counterparts. It's not my thing, but as Xavier's plus one, I have no choice but to go with him. Not showing up is a veiled insult.

"We're going."

A quirky smile lights his face. I think I was just played. Normally I'd be the one looking for an excuse not to go.

"Okay, babe. If you say so," he says.

Played. Oh, well. I score babe points. I can turn this up.

"Wings, chips and beer?"

"Just the usual, babe. Maybe the jalapeno chips."

He's back to his game and his warmth as the opposing team scores. I smile to myself knowing he'll make up for all my niceness on our weekend escape. And, he never disappoints.

Tom is back downstairs and stops by my side. For a minute I forget Bernadette and Bari the programmer are still here. He has to perform final calibrations.

"Looks   like   the   meet   was   successful. Congratulations are in order."

Bernadette motions with her fingers for me to sign off electronically on some paperwork.

"Initial here and there."

I do as she instructs and she looks over the electronic tablet one more time.

"Great. We're all set. I hope to see you in three months, to do this again."

"Fingers crossed. Thanks, Bernadette."

"My pleasure. Good luck."

She heads to her car and while I watch her start the gas guzzler her last words echo in my mind. Why would I need luck?

Bari approaches with his tablet and stencil. He has us to himself and looks Tom over from head to toe like a physical at a doctor's office.

"Hmm.   Gotta check one more thing.   WQRD-13552, convert to Dev Mode."

Tom's eyelids flutter as he stands still. Bari runs diagnostics and cross checks items on his tablet. "WQRD-13852, convert to Bay Mode. Cool. We're all synced and calibrated."

Tom blinks and walks away to attend to something.

"You're good to go, Ms. Greene," Bari says. "Before I forget, here's the latest manual, and shoes for when Tom leaves the house."

I take the drawstring and flash a polite smile.

"Thank you. Don't forget to revise the code."

"I'm on it. Already called a code review meeting. Gotta get back."

The truck retracts the protruding steps and close the elevator doors. Bari hurries to the truck. He slides into the front passenger seat and appears distracted. Quietly it pulls off and disappears down the street. If I'm not mistaken, I can still hear Bernadette's car as it gets on the 101.

5 HOMECOMING

Xavier and I sit together in the family room browsing the new holographic ComBorg manuals making comparisons of Kirk and Tom while the machine gets a full charge in his room. He forces Tom's shoes on his large feet.

"They're still creepy no matter how hard they try to make them more human. Maybe that's the problem. And you know what, it's really like having another guy in my girl's house, one with small feet. Sure you're not trying to tell me something?"

He swipes the manuals to the far right to turn them off and then reclines on the sofa. I stand to get to the kitchen.

"Fishing for a compliment, are we? Now that you mention it—I'd really like for my guy to be loyal, available to me at the press of a button, sleep in the next room when I feel like spreading out and not have a complex about his woman."

"A complex? When will this model be released again? Maybe I'll get the Halle Berry persona so you'll know how it feels to have an attention hogging machine taking what's rightfully yours. She'll be loyal, available when I need a drink and sleep in the chair in my room, every night."

My throat is parched so I head to the kitchen for a drink.

"You? Let a beautiful woman sleep in your chair, all night? I bet she'd be unrecognizable the next morning."

A flash of a scene across my mind stuns me. I'm motionless.

"Hey, you okay, babe?"

His tone changes from playful to serious.

"Babe."

I shrug it off.

"Just a little headache."

I regret the words the moment they leave my lips. It feels too soon to talk about the PHAC's notification or create another opportunity to talk about my cranial mesh.

"The nerve of that machine. Penal code blah, blah, blah," he says, mocking Tom's intonation.

"You're blaming the machine?"

"I mean, you're bringing a beta device to be tested and didn't check for stupid shit like Easter eggs? It used to be cute way back when but we've seen how it's just more code some jerk can mess with. What an asshole."

"They're just showing what they can do but it's an exploitation of people's personal information.   So fucking embarrassing. Sorry, hon. I'll bring it to the board. They ought to be spending their time testing rather than frivolous mini programs that adds no real value."

"I don't know. Maybe the concept can be useful in some other way.   Like telling a joke or something. Something positive, harmless."

I bring him a cold beer. He takes the bottle, pops the cap and takes a long sip. I straddle his lap and rest my chin on his shoulder.

"Yeah, but even some jokes can be inappropriate. Best to stick with the programming plan. Talking about a plan, what exactly did you mean when you said Tom was taking what's rightfully yours?" I say, nibbling his lobe.

"Nice try.   I saw what you did there trying to change the subject. When are you going to get checked? You can't keep putting it off hoping whatever it is will go away. You shouldn't be so affected by nightmares or be such a nervous wreck taking delivery of a machine that you get a headache."

There it is. The elephant in the room. I don't want to have this discussion again. These doctors look for any excuse to prescribe cybernetic augmentation like it's a cure-all. You feel a little down—get a cranial mesh with an anti-depressant drip.   Blurred vision—get bionic vision. Break an arm or leg, have a failing organ or   worsening   forgetfulness   and   there's   an augmentation for that too.   Slip, slip, sliding into machine land. Augmentation keeps the population in good health to rid it of frail humanity, but some of us have learned to value and cherish that frailty the more the human population edges towards extinction. I wish Xavier would give it a rest but he chooses to ignore the dangers of the black market.

I rest my head on his shoulder.

"Forget I said anything. You've been waiting for this day for so long to get a do-over. This time I'm here. It'll work out better." He puts the bottle down and gently hugs me then rubs my back. I sense he's tuned in to the game. "So, what happens next now that it's here?"

"He. The pronoun is friendlier than 'it'. He'll do the usual—organize my life. When he thinks he has fully charged he'll come downstairs and look for things to do, tasks to schedule, an inventory to catalog."

"Hey, Shelly. You looking good, ma."

I turn to see a face zoom on the holograph staring at us. I scoot back to sit beside Xavier while my cheeks return to their natural color.

"Hey, Habib."

Alek nods in a sly approval.

I swipe the microphone to the off position and glare at Xavier.

"Ma? What's that supposed to mean?"

"Babe. You need to relax. You know they're not like that. If anything, you're my horse."

"You're an ass."

I push him away and scoot to the end of the sofa.

"So tense. I'm joking. I keep forgetting to mute the darn thing and engage the viewshield. These guys are cool though. But you do look mighty cute when you sit like that."

"You know how I feel about my privacy. My body and what I do with it are my business. My thoughts and ideas belong to me, not to be mined and sold or used to further other people's self-serving agendas while I become afraid to live because every move I make is someone's datapoint or excuse to judge or invade my life. It's like stealing someone's soul."

"Gee, said I was sorry. I agree. I'm with you. You're even cuter when you're upset. Come here."

I'm almost sure the answer to the question he'd asked before whether Tom knew to only scan and sync with my systems was yes. The CB-X and all models before were built to be of service to one individual. Of course, with robot laws, there may be situations where Tom's loyalty could be overridden, but it's not in my nature to endanger any living thing, so there would never be a need for Tom to ever disobey me.

He looks so good. I want him to beg me back but lack the willpower to wait. I let myself fall onto his lap now that there wasn't an unintended audience. I nuzzle his nose.

"You're grounded, mister."

"For what?"

"You know."

"We should get a bigger place."

"And you need more room because?"

"It's beginning to feel crowded in here."

6 BETA

"**I**'ll be right back."

I need a minute to add some personal configurations to Tom to set my mind at ease. Xavier pulls up another game on holovision as soon as I'm out of sight. The man has season tickets and the arena's only thirty minutes away yet he's home with me.

"Yes!"

His team scores and I imagine he's widened the aperture to get a better view of the player's bench, interact with his favorite players and unmute the microphone to talk to his friends. I know I'm the one who scored but I need frequent reminders.

I head up to the guest room reserved for Tom. It was Kirk's room. I press the call button on my Pulsometer. It's a panic button if I should ever need his assistance, a new feature I suggested to the board that was adopted.

Though his steps are light, I hear him coming towards me in his normal gait. Two pushes would be an emergency, so he knows to act natural and to find me immediately.

"Shelly? Are you alright?"

The look of sincerity on his face is heart wrenching, like he's really capable of caring.

"We forgot to test the panic and emergency modes."

"Did I perform as expected?"

"You found me right away, you acted normally. You passed."

"There are new modules in my repertoire for you to enable and disable, as you see fit. Shall we schedule a day and time to review them?"

I walk him back to his room.

"What is Xavier doing, right now?"

"He's sitting in your family room watching the national basketball playoffs. He just sent a text."

"To whom?"

"His mother. A read receipt was delivered."

"What did it say?"

"He has an impenetrable firewall and encryption that hides the contents but I can make out the words 'mother and fine'."

"This conversation is confidential, understood. He should not know we discussed him and his text messages."

"I'm only loyal to you, Shelly."

7 RAPPORT

I don't even know why I asked Tom about Xavier. A part of me feels awful and another part is validating my need to protect myself. No one was without faults. No one was completely loyal. I hoped to find that loyalty. For now, I had it in Tom.

"My health module is completely in sync with your biorhythms and you appear to be in excellent human health for your age."

"Cool. Are we completely aligned then?"

"I'm afraid I'll have to learn more about you. You have an incoming emergency notification from the Public Health Advisory Council. Would you like me to play it for you?"

Shit. I forgot Tom is synced with all my electronic devices.

"Delete that message. Block all incoming notifications from that IP address and the PHAC."

"Are you certain you want to do that? How will you know if there's a new outbreak, if you're in the vicinity of an infected or virus shedding individual, if a prescribed medication has been recalled? The PHAC has made great strides keeping the population in good health."

"I'm not worried. The last major die-off was more than a decade ago. The humans left are highly resilient to known diseases. Please, do as I ask."

"Done. My sensors are picking up a cybernetic component nearby. Strange, I'm unable to sync with the device. I'll run the machine name against the IxTar database during my uplink."

"Thanks. That's all for now."

The drugstore comes into view. With Carisa disengaged my parking is atrocious but it's a quick errand for what, I don't know, but I will when I see it.

It's been a while since I drove myself or mingle with strangers in public or even browsed the shelves at a store, but this is something I have to do in person where I can closely see and touch my selections.

The drugstores have gotten smaller to reflect the dwindling human population—their only customers.

The choice to add-on cybernetics is becoming the de facto healthcare remedy rather than taking a pill and hoping it works without unexpected side effects.

My faceshield is set on its darkest levels as a disguise to give me the confidence I need. I'm sure I'm dropping datapoints I haven't thought of that are being sucked up by some public surveyor to be used for or against me at some later date but I have to see if there are pharmaceutical advances that could help me sleep better and lessen the headaches.

Two young human females exit the store happily giggling as they approach.

"She'll never find what she needs in there."

"Aug-men-tation," the other one says in a sing-song voice when I'm in earshot.

They're easy to spot—tall, thin, perfect dewy complexion, bone straight blond hair, vivid blue eyes, white teeth, well-proportioned extremities and overly confident. Products of genetic engineering these perfect humans walk amongst the defects without kindness and empathy. They stare as if they spot right off what's wrong or malformed. Are they better or are we worse off? Perfection is overrated.

I run back to Carisa. Never have I ever been happier to sit inside her protective walls.

Bari's holographic face fills the molecular confines of the pixelated screen.

"Can you backout a software upgrade from a cybernetic component?"

"It's possible. We do it all the time with ComBorgs and AI-enabled components but they're machines. The risks to a human or cyborg are too high and could result in permanent damage.   Wish I had better news. Someone you know?"

"Yeah. A friend."

"Wish I could help."

"No worries. Thanks, Bari."

"Anytime.   By the way, I forgot to mention that while in Beta the ComBorg's Dev, Stealth and Rogue interfaces are left open. We'll secure them leaving only the Bay mode operational once it goes public."

Tom's Bay mode is his default mode. Each mode is like a split personality, with its own segmented memories. They're unaware of the other's existence except for Stealth mode that sees everything and uses the best encryption and hacking algorithms to burrow through the deepest security layers.

"Cool. I hadn't noticed. You guys have done a terrific job so far. Thanks again."

"Good drive?"

His voice catches me off guard as he watches from the mudroom door. He'd time my usual exit from Carisa until I'm inside and felt something was off as I sat pondering my fate. There has to be a solution I can find on my own without alerting the entire world who'd be too happy to quickly slap a label on me and force their cure-all. No drugs, no software backout. I'm running out of options.

When in human history was a person ever afraid of losing themselves? How are these times better? Once the augment decision is made, it's final. There's no turning back. There'd be one less human. Who would I be?

Carisa's record of my little excursion is wiped with no traces left. I press the online button. All the lights on the dash, internal and external to the vehicle briefly shine before going dark. On the navigation is a seven-mile trip without a destination label. That's the one thing I couldn't erase. I pull myself together and exit.

"Hi."

"Hello, Shelly. You were offline for quite a while. Is everything alright?"

"Couldn't be better."

I slip past him to hang up my purse and coat and remove my shoes. His eyes rove my body trying to perceive my mood.

"I'm a good listener if you want to talk."

Talking to him in Bay mode is like having a personal discussion with a collective personality and all of IxTar. The thought is in the back of my mind having him live here, seeing and knowing everything Xavier and I do. Learning me. With my medical records stolen, my deepest thoughts are the only private things left.

But, it's not forever. Only three months and he'll return to IxTar with or without my stamp of approval. Tom is my job.

"Is Xavier happy?"

I did it again, blurting out a private thought intended to be kept inside. Maybe it wouldn't hurt hearing his take on one of the growing, annoying and bothersome issues I've kept to myself.

"He's often upset when his sports team lose or a player makes a move he doesn't agree with but when they score, he yells and screams. If the game makes him unhappy maybe he shouldn't watch."

"I assure you, watching the game if nothing else are some of the happiest moments of Xavier's life. The yelling and screaming are not from anger. They're frustration in good fun, that makes the game enjoyable."

"Telling the difference between fun-anger and anger-anger is very difficult."

"It helps knowing the source of the frustration to put anger and fun in the proper context."

"I see. Then to answer your question, Xavier is happy."

But is he happy with me, us? He never yells 'yeah, Shelly!' like he does watching his team score, and never say those three little words. So how could Tom ever know whether a human is truly happy? This deep human-level thought is unique to us. No machine would ever understand the complexities of the unspoken human interaction we hardly share out loud that's driven by our cares and fears. Inside us, is another inhabited world full of the human psyche that's constantly at work even in sleep. This unreachable realm is where the real governors of our existence deliberate the physical world. It's ground zero for determining our next actions to remediate our cares and fears. It's a well-protected fort to preserve our most delicate secrets. This is thoughtfulness, devoid of logic. There's no machine equivalent.

"Does Xavier make you happy?"

"Every day."

"Your neighbor seems unhappy?"

"Mr. Nardini?"

"He yells a lot. Is that why his wife and children left?"

"Mr. Nardini is going through a tough time. He was one of the first to report remote brain-hacking a few years ago. No one had heard of it so they thought he was crazy and cart him off to a mental hospital. He insisted he was the target of a high-tech bio-hack where he was bombarded with messages he was useless, that he was fired from his job and to kill himself."

"Sounds like Deathware."

"Figures. I've never heard of Deathware. I guess since there's Lifeware it would be a matter of time before its opposite was created. Anyway, Mr. Nardini conveniently left out how those messages started off friendly, helpful and useful and when he was hooked, they turned nasty, vile, evil. Others reported similar experiences. That's when it became clear foul play was involved."

"No wonder he often seems angry. Maybe a sport would make him happier?"

"Sometimes distractions help. He lost everything. They forced him to install a quantum cranial mesh in order to return home. No one will hire him since his ordeal is in public records. They think it's low frequency waves that were programmed to transmit messages directly to a targeted person's brain without them knowing."

"That's impossible."

"Sounds unlikely to me too but if you consider the human brain, how it's always seeking correlation and validation to justify thoughts and existence, maybe it could be hacked. The brain has so many unanswered questions it doesn't know how to stay silent. Maybe it sends out a beacon hoping for a response to the most fundamental: Why are we here? How is all this possible? What happens next? This could theoretically make it vulnerable to input tricking it to lower all security walls when it finds someone or something that reflects, answers or proves a thought. It becomes hungry for more, subscribing to that channel, listening without bias to get its validating fix. That opening makes it susceptible to other suggestive input from the trusted source; even ones that could cause harm. It's the same method used when anyone is trying to find a friend—we make ourselves vulnerable."

"Humans aren't that complex after all. They all want the acceptance of other humans."

"We've come a long way, Tom. Two million years on this planet and our tactics have evolved but our motives are pretty much the same."

"Is that why humans are better off with augmentation—so they'll be rid of this weakness?"

"Needing other people is a weakness?"

"I have no need for other machines."

8 THE NEW WORLD

"**S**helly? The car is waiting."

Like clockwork, the house smells of freshly brewed coffee and baked pastry. Something I once looked forward to is now mildly offensive.

"I'll be down in fifteen."

"Carisa says traffic is minimal and you'll arrive in time for your 10:15 with the AIC. I'll pack your breakfast for you to eat on the way."

"Thanks, Tom."

"Play headlines."

"The human population is holding steady as planned, said Sunil Paran, CEO of the Human Genomics Lab headquartered in San Fernando. 'Our mission ensures the continuation and moderation of the human species by only preserving and matching the best representations of the gene pool. We're proud to provide humans and cyborgs the opportunity to expand their

families in a private, holistic and respectable way without the inherent risks associated with childbirth, diseases, tainted biases and poor genetics'. The last census completed in January 2033 reports humans are 35% of the total population. The cyborg population has seen a steady growth, averaging 15% each year since. This growth in the cyborg transition has resulted in a dramatic correlated decline in crime and poverty within the United States. Many experts attribute this wellspring to the implementation of the Universal Basic Income and Healthcare Plan, commonly known as the UBI+HP. In other news, the massive Neuropharmaceuticals Inc. breach from a month ago has resulted in the Public Health Advisory Council accurately identifying all patients who used the private medical practitioner in the hopes of hiding their identities. The PHAC has contacted all victims of the breach with instructions to ensure their continued health and safety. The Hyper Swarm is being credited with saving the life of a human male in the Brixton neighborhood when his blood pressure suddenly rose leading to a heart attack. The quick dispatch of emergency personnel to his home who administered lifesaving measures was key to his survival. 'This is another example where open access to all medical records allowed us to administer the most effective treatment that prevented debilitating mistakes. We plead to the human public—use this as an example to consider cybernetic augmentation. It's safe and life changing. It could save lives.' Humans interested in learning how cybernetics could be of benefit, press 101 on your communication device to be directly connected with our knowledgeable and friendly representatives.

We'll be right back after this message from our sponsor, Quantometrics."

The computer's voice zone out as I quickly brush my teeth, wash, slap on my Pulsometer then pick out a comfortable outfit I put on before rushing downstairs.

"You look lovely, Shelly."

Tom holds out my usual sweater coat and I slip my arms in.

"Thanks. I'll be home a bit earlier for HalBorg's soiree so we'll skip dinner. Find out from Xavier what time he wants to leave and have his blue-gray Wexley's ready. See you later."

"He asked me to prepare your Van der Haans. Is that okay with you?"

My head is buried in the closet searching for a pair of shoes to match while I think how I can juggle my schedule. The AIC is an important coalition of disadvantaged young people from poor remote villages around the world who IxTar believe can help chart our course into the future. We're looking to mine the diamonds in the rough to differentiate ourselves, advance mankind through social responsibility and transform these young people's lives.

"That's fine. On second thought, plan an early dinner, 4 o'clock for eight guests. Three courses. Tell Xavier he can join us if he feels for an early dinner and company."

"Got it. I'll also rearrange the closet while you're away."

My schedule is packed from the time I wake up to the time I go to bed. I wondered what I would do with all the extra time freed up having a perpetual assistant. Now I know the answer.

Outside, the air is cool and crisp and the skies overcast. I slide into the passenger seat and take a sip of the coffee Tom prepared. My stomach churns then settle.

"Good   morning,   Shelly.   You're   absolutely glowing."

I forgot to put on my matte foundation in the hurry. Now I'm self-conscious my face appears oily. Maybe I should run inside and grab my makeup bag.

"Looks like we'll have a mild day today with a 20% chance of showers in the afternoon. The traffic is very light with a 10:05 ETA. Shall we go?"

"Hold for just a minute. I forgot something."

Carisa opens the door and Tom walks towards us with my purse.

"How'd you know?" I ask.

"Carisa."

"I'll send you the names and universal IDs of our guests when I get a moment. Be sure to validate their allergies against the menu."

We pull off onto the road. A few more inconspicuous electronic sensors have been installed near homes in the neighborhood for whatever purpose. Definitely to collect some type of data more so than to remedy low bandwidth internet connectivity.

Mr. Nardini is lost in the solitary act of clipping the edges of shrubs in his front yard. I wave. He doesn't look up. I wonder how he's really doing. They say no one has ever fully recovered.

The tree-lined street looks a lot neater since they removed the power lines and poles. Solar power concentrators are on the roofs of each home, some more noticeable than others as the technology evolve.

Sitting all the way back on the cushy leather seats I fight the urge to put my feet up while looking out the window at the sequoias and redwoods along the parkway. We get closer to the heart of the city with more traffic on the road and patrollers in the sky significantly increase.

"There's an accident up ahead."

Human error. At least that's the car maker's argument. Of course, the human driver will blame the machine. Every accident is thoroughly documented to determine root cause for improvements and this takes time, causing lengthy traffic jams like the ones I'm in. If human drivers would stay off the roads then it would be better for everyone.

"Shelly, I've just received a report of an emergency rolling black-out. All power along our route has been shut until the situation is corrected. I've contacted Tom and he's called your office to reschedule your 10:15."

Ugh. What's next? These power outages are commonplace even with an abundance of solar energy. Many companies who depend on machines and robots insist on nonrenewable energy resources for it takes time and capital to switch out the wiring and install the new energy source. As far as they're concerned, the mandate was met to convert 50% of energy to renewables by 2025 and they're on target to hit 100% by 2050. Besides consuming vast amounts of data, machines are a massive energy hog.

"There's an incoming."

"Thanks, Carisa."

Xavier's face appears on the hologram.

"Hey."

"You alright?"

"Um, yeah."

"Where'd you go yesterday?"

"What? Nowhere."

"Don't play with me, Shelly. Seven miles are unaccounted for on the trip calculator. Carisa didn't drive herself offline."

"It's nothing. I went for a drive. Got to exercise my driving muscles. If you don't use it, you'll lose it."

"And Reed's parking lot was just a fluke? I told you I've got connections. Don't think this is something you can do alone. I know how stubborn and headstrong you can be. You need to trust me."

"Fuck you, Xavier. I'm not your little project."

"Fuck me? See what I mean? The Shelly I know would never go from zero to sixty like that. It's getting worse. There. I said it. Now let's face it."

"I have to get to work."

"We're not done. We'll talk about it later whether you want to or not."

"End transmission."

Damn you, Carisa. Even offline you sold me out.

On scorchers like today, the city briefly shuts its electric power for 10 minutes to an hour to ward off recurring fires. They allow a number of fires because it's supposedly a natural event to germinate the redwoods. How can they claim to be green when they don't allow new trees to grow? The same fire-retardant trees are what they use to build homes in this area. The city would come to a screeching halt though if an outage persisted beyond the backup capabilities of generators and battery power.

"Connect me to Hazel."

The early birds are already at the office waiting for the meeting. Even if they were elsewhere nothing really stops us from meeting any time.

"Hazel Sanchez," she answers.

"Morning, Hazel."

"Hi, Shelly."

"I'm on my way to the office but might be a while and didn't want to reschedule the AIC. Can you get everyone to patch through to my Pulsometer?"

"Sure thing. Hold just a minute."

I widen a hologram to see the virtual team as they come online.

"Hello, Shelly. Caught in the outage."

"Just another day in the bay."

"At least we've got battery and solar. Let's give Dhobi an extra minute to join us. He's stuck in traffic somewhere."

Naveen is one of the cohorts from a rural Indian town who has taken on the de facto team lead role for the AIC. Sitting around him are Hajis, Pawindra, Xian and Tre. Security icons pop up over their heads with a light purple banner to indicate they're on foreign visas. Everyone has a unique identifier whether they are residents or visitors. In the universal database we know who they are, where they've travelled, their national rank and any information their home nation deems important for the public to know like education, tribe, allergies and non-sensitive private health or personal data. Open information ensures they are treated fairly, expeditiously and that their whereabouts are known. It ties into a global biometric system so everyone is identifiable anywhere on earth. Anonymity is largely a thing of the past. On their screen, a security popup displays above my head to verify I'm who I claim to be and all the information the Global Technology Council, a technology arm of the UN, has mandated to display for any electronic communication. Full name, universal ID, job title, current coordinates and IP address. This helps with security to identify imposters or bots and verify the individuals in attendance.

"Shelly, sorry I'm late."

"No worries, Dhobi. Glad you could join us. You're on auto-pilot, correct?"

"Yes, it's enabled. Morning, everyone. I see Naveen has corralled the rest of the team."

"Did you have your coffee yet? I know how moody you get without your java."

"Of course, you would, Naveen. How many times must I tell you I only drink tea," Dhobi answers.

"Alright, enough of the ribbing. Thanks, Hazel."

An audible beep sounds as the virtual assistant signs off.

"Looks like we're all set. So, what did we have on the agenda for today?"

"Pawindra was telling us this story from her village where they..."

"Naveen, she's right here. Let her tell us."

Pawindra puts her hands on the table and clasps them as she begins to speak.

The audio fizzles. The hologram renders malformed pixels before zooming out.

"Hello? Anybody there?"

"The connection has been lost. There are reports of sporadic outages and weather-related disturbances affecting communication devices."

"Thanks, Carisa. Hopefully it won't last all morning."

We pass the wreckage and one vehicle as suspected has a human driver. His dark skin is in direct contrast with the white sheet covering his body. A pressurized helmet preserves the last electronic currents in his brain to help with the transition to a full cyborg. The lead drone conducts an interview while the swarm collects evidence to build their report for the Autonomous Transportation Authority and the other agencies who will be furnished the data.

A series of beeps sound from Carisa's speakers.

"The ATA is requesting my records for the past two hours."

Because we're in the vicinity we might have useful information to piece parts of the accident together. We're obligated by law to furnish any video, images, or information that might be pertinent to the law authorities. Carisa enters recording mode the moment it drives on public roads and the data can be requested at any time or seized if denied.

"Permission granted."

My head pounds. Carisa pulls in and parks in my charging station in the IxTar garage. I take a last sip of my tepid coffee. I'm exhausted. There's nothing I'd like better than to turn around and go back home to bed but then I hate the feeling of wasting a day even more. Maybe Xavier won't mind going to the party without me. A glimpse of a well-dressed woman smiling and flirting with him in his well-fitted Wexley's fills my mind. Never mind, I'm going.

9 CHANGES

The day flies. I have Carisa pick me up at 3:15 to allow enough time to get home and skip the rush hour traffic.

Carisa slows as traffic comes to a halt at the entrance to the Golden Gate bridge. The lanes ahead on both sides are filled with pedestrians, a multitude all marching with cardboard banners and shouting in unison. Above, drones swarm and sirens holler in the distance as they try to get through.

A group of young men climb on the hoods of some cars. Others shake or pound the hoods of vehicles they're closest to while chanting or screaming words the windows have successfully muted.

"It's the Outliers. I've secured the doors and windows."

"Tell Tom I'll be a few minutes late."

"He's patching thru."

Tom appears as a hologram from my Pulsometer.

"Shelly, I'm getting reports of a massive protest heading your way. I've instructed Carisa to engage protective mode and secure the doors and dim the windows. Why don't they just do what's in their best interests and get augmented?"

I'm not in the mood for a lengthy existential crisis discussion with a machine but can't let his question go unanswered.

"Because being a full human is precious to them. They believe it's worth fighting for and will do anything to protect it. It's unreasonable to expect everyone to agree with the same things at the same time and I suppose that's why transitioning is optional to keep the peace but there shouldn't be a price to pay to stay human."

"There's no cost for augmentation. The government foots the bill for they know in the long run there will be cost benefits when an aging population no longer needs costly medications, medical care or expensive living arrangements."

"You've misunderstood what's meant by cost. While they live and breathe, right in their faces, their existence is being diminished to the point it looks like one day humans will no longer have free will. Some may see their needs, cares and fears problematic but to them that's what makes them human and they should not be forced to become cyborgs. To protect themselves these humans object to having their personal data freely shared with others without their consent and for that they have to pay extremely high prices for services out-of-pocket with a private practitioner or put themselves in danger buying services on the risky black market. Yes, if they opt-in to augmentation they receive no-cost medical care and a basic income but not too long ago privacy was a given right.   Outliers believe they're entitled to it and shouldn't have to give it up in exchange for a better life and will fight to get things to change. For that they'll suffer."

"Then they choose to suffer."

"I don't expect a machine to understand what it means to be human, to have deep rooted values, and to fight for their beliefs but if that's what you mean by suffer, then yes, it's what they've chosen. Still, they should be treated equally as cyborgs, not forced into becoming one if they choose to oppose cybernetics, not muted as much as possible and have difficulty finding and maintaining livelihoods.   They deserve to be heard."

"I don't understand, why do they have trouble finding work?"

"To stop them from pursuing litigation. If they have no money, they have no power. If their data is taken, the lesser power they'll have.   They see themselves becoming dependent on a system they'll need to live, a system that governs every aspect of their existence. That dependence is a trap that becomes an addiction and addiction is a weakness."

"Resistance is futile."

"What'd you say?"

"It's a saying, when someone expends energy opposing the inevitable."

A swarm of drones fly low above us. Canisters of a gaseous substance explode as they hit vehicles and the surrounding roads. A fog emerges, covering everything on the bridge. The Outliers scream and run in the opposite direction. A face appears at the rear passenger window beside me. The woman pounds on the glass, screaming, mouthing muted words.

"Open the door."

I can't tear my eyes away from her contorted face.

"Shelly, some of these Outliers are violent."

"Carisa, open the fucking door and let her in."

I engage my faceshield.

The woman's eyes are bloodshot, tearing, puffy. Her round belly protrudes through her brown coat. She coughs while scooting onto the seat in front of me. I hand her a towel.

"Thanks. You didn't have to."

I force myself not to roll my eyes or stare at her middle.

"Where can we drop you?"

Xavier would be mad as hell if he knew I harbored an Outlier.

"Are you passing Bay Street?"

"Carisa, head to Bay Street."

"So, you're really one of them?"

"What do you mean?

"I know who you are. You should be on our side after that machine you owned went crazy. What did you sell your soul for—a new arm, bionic leg, perma vision, that chip they implant in people's skulls so they no longer need a secondary education? Look around. Nothing but robots and machines. What about the sanctity of being human? When did that lose its value?"

Humans can't keep up unless they're augmented. I could tell her this, but why add gas to the flames? It's the truth I'm still forcing myself to accept.

"They look on us like we're invalids, the diseased, just waiting for us to croak so they can finally have their way. No way. The world's gone to hell."

Carisa stops at a light near Bay Street.

"We could drop you where you live, if you want."

"What are you smoking? After the protest? Every single person walking on that bridge is now listed as a POI. Where's the first place you think they'll look?"

"Are you hungry? I could fix you something at my home..."

She grabs the handle to the door and pushes it open. "I'd rather starve than take a handout from a sell-out. Thanks for the ride."

She throws a dollar bill on the seat and slams the door.

I'm intrigued at the relic, slowly unfolding to reveal the face of a revered figure. I hadn't seen a paper bill in years. It's now a collectible. My mind wanders thinking how difficult life is for this woman and what kind of life her child will have once its born. She's fighting for what she believes. There's nothing worse than someone who has lost the will to fight.

"Let's go home, Carisa."

A light mist fills the cabin to sanitize the surfaces.

A relentless drum beats in my head.   The cool compress brings little relief. I reach for the base of my skull to feel the only telltale sign of an embedded cranial mesh. The air makes waves that move in and out like I'm in a desert seeing a mirage. I reach to touch the visual distortion but my fingers go through air.

A notification on my Pulsometer beeps. I thought I'd opted out of unsolicited newsfeeds. The words cranial mesh catches my attention. No one should have known I have one or of my interest. Maybe its random. My inclination is to request I be removed from their distribution list before deleting but I hesitate. Opening it is pretty much expressing my consent and interest but I can't fight the urge to know who knows or suspects. I want to know what it says. At least it's better than typing the words in a search engine where it would be blasted to any number of advertisers and then linked to my online profile. Instead of opening I locate the sender meta data and get their IP address. It's owned by Neuropharmaceuticals located in the Bay area. The point of contact is Dr. Sundstrom Armsby. The neuropathologist who installed my cranial mesh.

4:30 rolls around and the notification is still on my mind. Another beep sounds from my Pulsometer. My clenched fist and teeth burrow through my flesh seeing the notification is from PHAC. How could Tom not do as I ask? Breathing in I slowly relax. Maybe they're using another server not in my blocked list to send their messages. The subject: Final Notification. I hope so.

Dr. Armsby could help. Putting Carisa in offline mode, I take the wheel.

Ten minutes later the familiar brick building comes into view. Three stories, brightly lit, the parking lot deserted except for four vehicles. I drive around the outside to see if maybe the occupants were parked on the other side. Empty, except for one car. A man's silhouette briefly lingers then pass by a window on the second floor. I recognize the oddly shaped head and pointed nose. The light dims.

Exiting the offline Carisa, I make my way to the elevator, press the 2nd floor button. The excuse I thought of is ready to go if anyone asks what I'm doing there. The sound of a door shutting halfway down the hall rattles me. A red light comes on above the door. The light in the hallway briefly dims.

His distinctive voice echoes through the wood door. A woman asks a question and Dr. Armsby respond. With my body leaning against the door the voices are clearer.

"Why don't you give it a shot, Ms. Winters."

"I'm a little nervous. So much can go wrong with a cranial mesh," she says.

"Oh, you'll do just fine. Removing is a cinch. The neurobot is even more adept than I and I've been doing this for years."

I'd give anything to see this, to be assured this is something I want to do. Another door is nearby. I approach and see it isn't closed. A gentle push and I'm inside looking at chairs on one side and a glass pane the full length of one wall that shows Dr. Armsby's room.

Although dimly lit, Dr. Armsby is accompanied by two students, and a medical robot. A human patient lies unconscious on the gurney. A holographic picture of a brain is projected on a wall with a diagram of a cranial mesh superimposed. The text is too small to read.

"The patient is registered and prepped. The neurobot is ready," says Ms. Winters.

"With anesthesia or without?" the neurobot says.

"With."

Leading the procedure, the neurobot does just about everything while the assistant stands nearby to supply various instruments and keep an eye on the patient's vitals. Dr. Armsby and the other student gives them room.

"Commencing Incision," the neurobot says.

Ms. Winters hands the machine a sharpened medical blade.

Skillfully, the neurobot makes an incision at the base of the patient's skull. The tiny white tag of the cranial mesh is revealed. Ms. Winters takes the blade and places it in a metal pan and hands the neurobot a tray with an absorbent material. The neurobot takes one and uses it to remove some drainage. Ms. Winters holds out the pan for the neurobot to dispose of the used bandage.

"Confirm vitals," the neurobot says.

"Vitals steady."

"Commencing Removal."

Holding onto the cranial mesh's tag the neurobot gently pull the device until it clears the tiny incision and is completely removed. The pliable device is placed in a separate pan held out by Ms. Winters.

"Removal complete."

The neurobot proceed with suturing the patient and confirming vitals one last time.

The entire procedure is less than ten minutes. Dr. Armsby lifts the cranial mesh with gloved hand and inspects it.

"We look for any unusual wear and tear that could indicate an adverse state of the device and make a note of it to send to the manufacturer. Both chips look to be in good condition."

"Why would they make a device for a human that has a cyborg chip?"

"So there's no need for invasive surgery when the patient decides to transition. Every cyborg has a cranial mesh they use for interconnectedness, communication and data processing. It's optional for humans. The human chip is the one most frontal. Its purpose is simple: checks dopamine levels and release a micro dose to calm the wearer as needed. The cyborg chip is the latter. Note how it's a bit larger, more complex in design. The chamber holds cortisol and other neurochemicals to temper emotions. Software works with the cyborg chip to control how atoms reform themselves into an expansive network of carbon nanotubes used to dispense neurochemicals deeper and to the furthest regions of the brain that requires it. But this is what truly makes a human a cyborg, a superhuman genuine-intelligenced being. This is what saves man from truly going extinct."

"If the cranial mesh didn't have both chips then that bad software upgrade wouldn't have switched the dormant cyborg chip on in human patients. I think it's bad design. "

"Well, we have to start somewhere. Humans don't have a cyborg master chip where the fail-safe is located that could have prevented this medical crisis. A switched-on cyborg chip expects to find a cyborg master chip to pair with but when it doesn't find one the device goes wild creating multiple nanotubes with the intent of jumpstarting an electronic connection. Eventually it overheats, decimates and fries the human's cerebrum."

"Ouch."

"That's the dark side of a cranial mesh in humans. Otherwise, it's a remarkable device, a medical and technological wonder. These chambers are in good shape. Nothing unusual here. Prepare it for hazardous disposal. The patient will have minor hemorrhaging for a few hours, a mild headache and after a few weeks of adjustment, good as new. Well done, Ms. Winters."

"Thank you, Dr. Armsby."

"Revive Mr. Cartwright and call it a night. Mr. Nesbitt will get a crack at his patient first thing in the morning."

"Looking forward to it, Dr. Armsby. Was the anesthesia really necessary for such a simple outpatient procedure?"

"It's a precaution, but not necessary for adult patients who can lie still without moving for the duration."

"Dr. Armsby, seeing how easy it was to remove the cranial mesh is there a chance patients could attempt this themselves without coming in to the facility?"

"I don't see that being a possibility. I mean, they'd have to be under some duress to even think about it. Self-removal could cause significant harm to a cerebrum if not done properly or mechanical death to a cyborg. Off to make my report. With the data breach and having to report every new removal to the PHAC, we must be cautious as we can't take another infraction. They'll shut us down and we don't want that to happen. I'll be in my office. You two can finish up."

"Good night."

The door opens and I listen as his footsteps fade down the hall. The students clean up and wash their hands. Ms. Winters approach the neurobot and look it over.

"Suspend Anesthesia."

"Anesthesia suspended."

After a minute, Mr. Cartwright sits up on the gurney awaking from a short but deep sleep.

"How do you feel?"

"Fantastic. That was fast."

"Removal was a success. We'll give you a few minutes to get dressed."

After waiting five minutes I'm sure the halls are empty. My heartbeat kicks like a stallion galloping at high speed. I leave the facility seeing I have no need to speak to Dr. Armsby.

Carisa and I linger along the pier. It's a safe popular spot to bring Carisa online so as not to arouse Xavier's suspicion of an unaccounted for trip. A few miles will be unaccounted for but I'll feign ignorance if he asks. After driving around for half an hour to finalize my plan, I head home.

By 7, the hum of the house starts to get on my nerves. Everything seems to be connected to an internal or external source to function, to get more data or energy to operate. I swear I can hear Tom's inner machinations—a constant whir interrupted by a gentle rumble—over and over like clockwork. Xavier will be home soon to liven the place, add his own internal and external music to the dullness. My face feels hot and sticky so I return to my room to wash up. Beads of sweat form on my temple as the room spins. Lightning cracks my skull.

"Tom?"

I want to say his name but my lips won't move, sound won't come out.

I press the panic button on my Pulsometer before my extremities go numb.

"The IxTar medics are scanning you. Hold on. You hear me, Shelly?"

Everything is black.

Twinkling specks of light appear throughout the dark. It's quiet and I'm floating. *Breathe.* I want to breathe but don't remember how. *Breathe. Get up.* A speck of light explodes filling the dark. I'm hurled into bright white light.

Tom and a hologram of an IxTar medic hovers over me.

"All readings are normal. We'll run some tests and let you know our findings. We'll be on standby if needed."

"Tom."

"You fainted. A heat stroke probably. It's 110."

"AC?"

The ability to form full sentences takes effort. Medic. Scan. It's a matter of time before aggregated datapoints form my story.

"Don't tell Xavier."

"Certainly, you're not planning on going out after this?"

"It'll be okay."

The door bell rings. Outside a patrol drone flies low and pause above the house.

"It's the metro force.   They're scanning the property."

"You called the medic. They work together, Tom. Answer the door."

Yet another datapoint or two.

I scramble to my feet and follow him but he moves with speed and agility.

"Good evening. We got a report of a disturbance. Everything okay?"

"Yes, sir. Everything's fine."

"Mind if we come in and take a look?"

"My human is resting and doesn't want to be disturbed. Everything's fine."

"We're just doing our jobs. Where's your human?"

I drag my body to the catwalk overlooking the foyer and slowly make my way down to the top landing.

"His human is right here. He said everything is fine, Officers. Thank you and good evening."

Tom closes the door.

"Pushy, aren't they?"

"They know this house better than I do. It's beyond me why they need to come inside when they can see every square inch from the outside. I'm heading back up."

"Would you like me to fix you anything?"

"I'm fine. Turn up the AC."

"The privacy barrier is resetting now that the emergency has timed out."

"You did good, Tom. Where's Xavier by the way?"

The front door shuts as soon as I enter my room. Tom freezes, stopped by the privacy barrier.

"He's just arrived."

"Hey, babe. Where's everybody?" Xavier calls.

I rush to the ensuite.

"Shower on. 65 degrees."

I strip and jump in.

He opens the door and it shuts behind him.

I close my eyes and stand beneath the steady stream of cool liquid. The nausea fades and I'm more myself. A cool air covers me. A lemony musk fills my nostrils and quickly fade. I'm embraced by lean muscular familiar arms. Gentle hands run the length of my chest and cradles me. A warm body shields my back and neck from the cool water.

"Babe. You know…"

I don't want to put space between us but it's for our own good. We've gambled before and thankfully have been lucky but one of us have to be the adult and follow the rules, no matter how unnatural.

"Sorry I lost my temper earlier.   But babe, how many times must I tell you we're in this together?"

The words are what I want to hear, our rift has passed, but a part of me want to know I solved my own problem. His hands caress my skin. He loses himself in me. I pull away.

"This is fucking ridiculous. Consenting adults can't do what the hell they want in their own house. Why not?"

"Ask the Minister of Health."

"Where's the joy?"

"That's the point. Joy is forbidden. Did you see any joy in the minister's face when he proclaimed: 'There are safer and more fulfilling ways to preserve the humanoid population where the outcome is known and the centuries old dilemma of sin, rampant disease transmission and wasteful distraction of the human intellect is eradicated'?"

"Bullshit. They want us all to be fucking cyborgs with the pretense of preservation. C'mon, Babe. Not even a little?"

"Not even."

"He didn't say anything about sin."

"I know. But it's like we're in the dark ages."

"What's a man to do when he's in dire need of a little fun with his woman."

"He stops whining and moaning trying to get his way; forgets his carnal desires and immerse himself in the theatrics of the eccentric. If we don't hurry, we'll be late for HalBorg."

"Bummer, when someone redefines your fun. You know what it's like?"

"What?"

"Being dressed by your parents in what they think is fashionable. I so miss you."

"And I miss you. But one wrong step and they'll sic Shameware on us calling us out everywhere we go. It's not worth the public humiliation if we... get caught."

His strong arms pull me close.

"Fine. Another hug?"

It takes self-control to not give in but like any other emotional rush, it'll pass, at least for me.

"All my hugs are yours, but we better get going."

"Lohan is a party freak. He'll be showing off all night as long as he's got guests."

"Hmm. The chick in the slinky black dress is going to be very disappointed if you're not there for her to flirt with."

"What? Who?"

"Just some sexy bitch who'll try to make a move on you. I can't wait to see the look on your face when she grabs you."

"I have all I need right here."

"Yeah, but is it everything you want?"

I roll over and take a peek at my Pulsometer. 115 degrees. It's late. We should have left an hour ago but Xavier and I, it's like we're made for each other. In his arms the whole world melts away. I snuggle deeper in his chest to bury the little guilt pangs. That's one reason I'm hesitant to remove my cranial mesh, just in case it's why I can't get enough of him. What if the safety I've found in his arms is all a chemical illusion? What if it turns out I don't truly love him? How lonely and cold this world would be.

"Babe."

"Hmm."

"We should at least make an appearance."

"I don't want to."

"Come on. You'll hate yourself in the morning if you don't make the effort. Your Wexley's look mighty lonely without you in it."

"Alright. Five more minutes. Promise."

Five minutes have a way of turning into fifty.

I pull the covers away and run to the ensuite.

He gives chase.

"Shower on. 100 degrees. Dim light."

"System malfunction. Water not available."

He grabs my waist and kisses my lips.

"Hmm. I can't believe this is all mine."

"And the state's."

"Fuck. No fair. They need to get the fuck out my bedroom."

"Feisty. There are other things we can do."

"Shower on. 90 degrees."

"System malfunction. Water not available."

"What's going on—no water?"

"This better not be happening."

Thirty minutes later we're dressed in our finest. Daphne picks us up and drives to the hidden mansion off Cabrillo.

"Daphne, stay on the Xernet and block all attempts to join the public domains."

The tree-lined driveway wrapped in twinkly white lights is barely wide enough for two cars to pass. Quarter mile from the turn off the lights on the home come into view. Every single window is lit and every step has a strip of light to contrast the darkness.

"There's a private message I'm to let you out here and proceed to the east wing for parking."

"Thanks, Daphne. We'll be about an hour. Get a charge if you can."

"Enjoy your evening."

Another vehicle pulls up behind us and an expensively dressed couple exits.

Xavier takes my hand and we take the throng of stairs to arrive at the grand entrance. Couples are in each other's arms along the sides drinking champagne, laughing or talking animatedly. Festive music fills the air as the double doors opens and close as people comes and goes.

"Is this a home?"

"He lives here a few months out of the year."

"Imagine the upkeep."

The foyer is exaggerated spanning the three levels with a barrel domed glass ceiling that extends to the back of the home. Round giant chandeliers are suspended like mini suns. Rich dark paneled woods line the walls to separate the east and west wings. Exquisite creamy marble floors add a vivid contrast against the dark walls and luxurious silk and velvet tufted benches and chairs are strategically placed for the greatest impact among tall verdant bamboos and expansive palms. Matching curved staircases are partially exposed leading to the upper levels. On one side halfway through, a raised platform with a live band and singer has the attention of most of the guests.

On the ground level, an immense bar with a waterfall as a backdrop busily serves and mixes up drinks. Guests sit on the back stairways to their respective wings while others dance in the space between the band and bar.

Xavier and I make our way through until we get to the wall of giant French doors leading out to the columned rear portico. Tables are decorated with fancy napkins, flatware and black tablecloths while guests are served mini entrees by uniformly dressed waiters and waitresses.

"Hungry?"

"Maybe later. We should find Lohan so he knows we're here."

"Oh, he knows. Not much escapes HalBorg."

"Wanna dance?"

He takes my hand and lead me to the dance floor. I'm not a big fan of dancing but in Xavier arms I don't really care if I'm offbeat. Quietly I'm calculating the minutes until we're ready to leave. Forty-six. A man taps Xavier's shoulder and he turns. We release each other as he embraces Lohan. I recognize him from his picture in the technology e-gazines.

"Vinson, thought that was you. Glad you could make it."

"Wouldn't miss it. Shelly, Lohan. Lohan, this is the woman who keeps me on my toes literally and figuratively."

"Indeed. I've been dying to meet the woman he can't shut up about. Welcome, welcome."

"Thanks. It's always awkward meeting someone you've heard about, seen on the news, in person. I'm a big fan, by the way. Your yAIs are simply genius."

"I'm glad you think so.   Vinson says you're at IxTar."

"A product consultant."

"A techie at one time, though.   Wouldn't mind stealing you away. HalBorg could do with your talent."

"Lohan, always the business man.   Shelly is committed to IxTar for sentimental reasons. Believe me, if she wasn't, she'd be working for me."

"I'm not giving up that easy.   By the end of the evening I'll find a way to change her mind?" He smiles, winks and pats Xavier on the back. "We must have tea, soon. If you don't mind me saying, you're absolutely radiant."

"Watch it, HalBorg."

"Lucky dog. Ah, to be young and in love again. Enjoy the party."

Lohan walks to mingle with other guests while Xavier resumes our dance.

"What was that? You didn't tell me the two of you were that close."

"We went to school together. He was an upper classman and the president of our frat."

"It's like I hardly know you, Xavier Vinson."

"Can't divulge all my secrets. Then I'd bore you to death. How about a drink?"

"Sure. I'll meet you at the bar. Just got to…"

I need to check my makeup and freshen up a bit.

"What do you want?"

"Ginger ale."

He smiles, and heads to the bar.

I'm too embarrassed to ask where's the lady's room so I look for a room other women are entering and leaving. Finally, I locate it next to the valet taking coats. The giant dark wood door opens to a small vestibule that leads to another room. I turn the handle on the door and everything inside is gold except for the marble walls but floors, sink, commode glow from the light of a dimly lit chandelier. The room is large, warm and comes with a live attendant. She politely smiles and exits the room. While she stands guard, I take my time to fix a stray hair, and adjust my lipstick. Ugh. My cheeks are a little too puffy. I look away from the mirror and turn the tap. No water. The woman gently knocks before entering and presents a moist towel for me to wipe my hands.

"Thanks."

It's awkward as I don't have a way to tip so I smile again. She holds out a gold tray for the used towel and opens the door for me.

Xavier is deep in the crowd, way at the other end of the room. A swirling light comes on dappled with tiny spotlights. Epic music begins to play. People look around to see what's going on, before crowding to the rear staircases. Lohan wears a microphone, the lights in the room are dimmed further and a spotlight shine on him. He looks quite the entertainer in his white dinner jacket as he takes a spot in the center of the room. Cheers and claps fill the room like this is something they were waiting for.

"Thank you. Thank you. Thank you all for being my guests."

Xavier pick up our drinks at the bar. A woman sidles very close to him, whispers something in his ear. He shifts uncomfortably. She grins, whispers again and walk towards the crowd. He doesn't see me yet.

"HalBorg prides itself on the ability to design and offer our customers the best in artificial intelligence personas. Our yAI model is far outpacing our closest competitors and we're ready to leave them in the dust. If it's one thing we've learned from our sordid past is to treat each other with kindness. So why make machines with increasing intelligence to surpass ours and treat them with a submissive mentality? What would that teach them or say about us? Now, as you know we're based on the premise of digital personas that goes where you go, that looks, sounds and acts just like you, but better, faster, smarter. But even HalBorg knows there is nothing like a body to mimic real human relationships and that's why we're proud to introduce the next line of HalBorg's yAI. Ladies and gentlemen, the future, the HalBorg bodyAI."

"What took you?"

Xavier hands me a glass. He seems bothered.

"Sorry. You ok?"

I take a sip.

"Fine."

"Who was that woman?"

"You mean the groper?"

No way. That was a wild ass guess he'd run into such a person.

People push past us to get a closer look. Spotlights shine on each of the rear staircases. A commotion breaks out. HalBorg leads the procession as multiple clones of him all dressed alike animatedly wave and descend the stairs to mix with the gasping and enthralled crowd.

"Now, I'll donate a million dollars to the first person who correctly identifies the real me."

The spotlight leaves HalBorg and return to the dual staircases.

"To make your evening a bit more entertaining I've brought some friends," HalBorg voice echoes over the microphone.

A well-dressed man and woman descend the lit stairs on one side.

"Oh my gosh!"

"Amazing!"

"Who is it?"

Another couple follows closely behind them, walking slowly, smiling and nodding to the crowd.

"The likeness is unbelievable."

"He's outdone himself."

"Genius."

"He's done it again."

I recognize Xavier's voice and feel his cheek brush lightly against mine. He pulls me closer and whispers.

"He's unstoppable. You recognize her?"

The woman is dressed in an elegant white ball gown and walks with an air about her. She's gorgeous.

"No, who is she?"

"Maybe a little before your time. Hard to believe they're machines, huh?"

Those are the bodyAI? They look like rich snooty people from a long-ago rat-pack era.

"IxTar really has some tough competition. These models are fantastic."

"There's a reason he's the goat. IxTar has its work cut out. HalBorg is relentless."

Another pair ascends the stairs and the guests are caught up in the excitement as they interact with the machines.

"Is that Churchill?"

"This tech could have helped him out when he was hiding his stroke from the queen and the public. He could have carried on business as usual and Eisenhower wouldn't be able to tell the difference."

"Babe, we're at a party. Fun time, remember?"

"Sorry. That looks like Bogart. Is that Kennedy? Monroe? And that one...I can't remember her name, from the breakfast movie."

"Stephanie. No, that's not it. There's enough data on all of them in the archives. Mannerisms, voice, life stories only help to bring them back to life. It's like that wax museum, only interactive."

"Wonderful, isn't it?"

The groper stands close to us, hitching up on Xavier's side like they're old friends. It takes every ounce of self-control not to throw my drink in her face but I understand there's a shortage of real men, human males. Her black slinky dress clings to every curve on her svelte body. Her eyes rove Xavier.

"Keep your filthy hands to yourself."

Xavier tightens the hold on my arm but I'm not sorry. Our eyes meet. I step in front of Xavier to stand directly in front of her. She doesn't budge.

"Hmm. He didn't seem to mind."

Xavier's hold on my arm hurt. I ignore it and I'm in her face.

"He's a gentleman. Now step off."

More bodyAi walk down the stairs while the first ones are mingling with the crowd. Lohan and his clones mill about like a proud tech pioneer.

Groper is whisked away by a lurking admirer.

Xavier leans into me and whispers.

"Halle might be coming sooner than expected."

I pull away.

"You're not her type. Look, I'm not in the mood to play 'get your girlfriend jealous'. That's just camp. Ready?"

"B-but, it's just getting started."

"We agreed on one hour."

"Alright. Let's go. I think we caught the highlight. Sure you're okay?"

Outside, Lohan inspects a concept car driven by a celebrity. He approaches us while Xavier summons Daphne to pick us up.

"Leaving so soon?"

His swagger reeks wealth, ego and confidence.

"We have an early morning. It was fun. Thanks for the invite."

He nods at the celebrity and turns to give us his full attention. Give me, his full attention.

"I'll bet anything you have some useful ideas my team could use to improve the bodyAIs. IxTar will be done in a matter of years. Humor me. Name your price."

I've never met a man fuller of himself. Xavier pulls me closer.

"Looks like you're doing fine all by yourself, Mr. HalBorg."

He flashes a smile to reveal perfect white teeth. Ugh. Perfection is so overrated.

"Well, you know what they say, 'It's only the one on top who truly loves what he does'."

Xavier gently pulls me away as Daphne opens its doors to let us in.

"You got it wrong, HalBorg. It's the one who chooses to stay on the bottom."

"Ah, touché. You'd have to be on top once in your life to know."

"So, which one was the clone?"

His eyes pierce mine.

"All of them, my friend. All of them."

"Did he get the proper signoff?"

"What signoff?"

"The bodyAI, all those personas HalBorg emulated, isn't there some right the families or estates hold in marketing their likeness? IxTar licensed the personas of the celebrities they use in their ComBorgs."

"That may be the ethical thing to do because it was required at one time but now no one entity can claim sole ownership of a word or likeness, be it an object or a lifeform. It falls within the public domain in the interest of continuous innovation. HalBorg is at liberty to use any number of likenesses in his bodyAi."

"It's understandable that a grieving family might commission HalBorg to create a bodyAI in the likeness of their loved one but free rein to recreate a monster from our history? And even if it's someone that had good character, what if this unsanctioned bodyAI is programmed to do and say things contrary to the individual's beliefs, or their existence prolongs the grief of their loved ones? What recourse do they have?"

"Augmentation. The cure-all."

"How could I forget? Emotions are bad, a weakness, that must be dulled and removed. But it's what makes us independent. No wonder they want it gone with all these new anti-human, pro-cyborg policies popping up every other day."

"And they're winning."

"Where are we headed, babe?"

"To forever."

My Pulsometer shows 2:15AM. Xavier snores gently. It's now or never. There's nothing to take with me, except for my courage and Tom. It's past curfew, but it isn't illegal to have a nervous breakdown. I had to have the excuse ready, just in case I'm stopped by a patroller.

Tom comes online and looks up when he senses I'm passing his room. Quietly he dislodges from his charging station and follows behind me. I head for the front door. Carisa's lights come on and doors are opened.

"Offline mode."

I take the driver's seat and motion for Tom to take the front passenger seat.

Daphne's lights come on briefly sensing proximity motion.

"Where are you going at this hour? Everywhere is closed."

"Remember our talk about loyalty?"

"I'm loyal to you, Shelly."

"Right. Here's your chance to prove it."

"What do you need me to do?"

"Don't ask any questions. Just do as I say. Got it?"

"But what if I have questions?"

"You will."

"Why isn't Xavier coming?"

"You're doing it, Tom. Stop it with the flipping questions. Capisce?"

"Are you angry-angry or fun-angry? Sorry."

I look out the window and bite my tongue.

"Hands on the wheel; eyes on the road. Xavier says he should be notified..."

"Don't let me take your ass back to IxTar. You know what those programmers would do on my command? Backspace. Every single line of code. For you have clearly forgotten why you're here."

"I'm sorry."

I take a deep breath. Maybe this is a mistake. But maybe it isn't.

"Look, Tom. I've been under a lot of stress lately. I'm the one who should be apologizing. I had no right to speak to you that way, it's just that, I need your help with something important, okay. Your help. Not Xavier's."

The building comes into view. There's one car parked overnight so I pull in beside it.

"WQRD-13552, convert to Dev Mode."

Tom's eyelids flash and a haptic let's me know he's ready. He'll have no memory of our little outing.

I exit Carisa and walk to the passenger door to open it for Tom.

"Follow me."

He follows silently and complicit as we approach the building. The doors are unlocked. Inside we take the elevators to the second floor and approach the room Dr. Armsby and his students were using hours earlier. Inside the actual room feels so much different than being a spectator. The neurobot awakes from its power saving mode and comes online.

Tom stands around like a robot awaiting his next set of instructions.

"I need you to do as the neurobot says. If there's something you don't understand, ask for clarification."

I gather all the medical equipment into a metal pan just as Ms. Winters did and place it on a table beside the bed. The start button is in the upper right of the neurobot's thin metallic shoulder. A gentle touch and it blinks ready.

"What's the procedural code for a cranial mesh removal?"

"More information is required," it says.

"What information do you need to proceed with a cranial mesh removal?"

"Patient's universal ID."

"That's it?"

"A Universal ID has all the information required to perform the relevant calculations and ensure all safety measures are taken."

"HG-113-LR-0496," I say.

"Retina Confirmed. Cranial mesh removal authorization obtained. Preparing for cranial mesh removal. With anesthesia or without?"

"Without."

"Your next of kin has been notified. Please lay face down on the table."

"Who's my next of kin?"

"Xavier Vinson is listed as next of kin."

Fuck. Thank god he's asleep. By the time he gets the notification this will be long over.

My head slips into the indentation on the table to expose my neck. The neurobot approach and pins my hair out of the way. A cold gel is squeezed on my skin then wiped clean.

The lights dim and I pray this will be over quickly.

"Commencing incision."

"Commencing incision."

Tom stands motionless.

"Tom, the blade."

"Please lie still."

"Commencing incision."

The door blasts open.

"What the hell is going on in here?"

I'm afraid to move. Gently I lift my head from the table and turn to face the voice. The woman's eyes tear through me. The recognition is instant. It had been a while since we'd seen each other in person. Public and private hospitals are being actively phased out so she'd taken a post at a private medical facility where invasive and outpatient surgeries are performed. Patients convalesce or recover in the privacy of their homes with a watchful and well-trained medicbot that's a nurse, pharmacist and hospice rolled into one.

"Shelly? What are you doing in here and at this hour?" She enters the room and look around. "That's Dr. Armsby's medical equipment."

"Hey, Viola," I say, sitting up.

"No, no. Don't hey Viola me. I wanna know what the hell you think you're doing? "

"Um, removing something that's bothering me."

"Let me guess. You have a cranial mesh?   No wonder you're always so fricking happy when the rest of us are bitching about our lives. Girl, uhuh. This isn't right. Let Dr. Armsby do his job. This neurobot was just about to cut you the heck up. Who's that?"

"Tom. My new assistant."

"Another one?   You think this machine can do everything? You think it could save you if this neurobot cut the wrong artery?   Girl, you're lucky I decided to come in early. You lucky it's me. You're a damn fool thinking a removal procedure is that easy."

It looked easy.

"I just don't need the whole world knowing my business, alright."

"You still on that privacy shit? So what if they know? You not the only one fighting hard to keep her shit together. At least you got it right the first time and got it installed. But, you off the rails, girl. Maybe the shit is malfunctioning for you to get the nerve to go this far. Lie down."

"What?"

"Lie your ass down. Ought to slap you silly. Let me run a diagnostic check on this mesh. How you been otherwise?"

"A nervous wreck. Waiting for this mesh to fry my brain. Working through crazy shit I can't explain."

"Hmm. Like what?"

"Suspecting Xavier. Bouts of mirages. Doing stupid shit."

"First off—Xavier? Don't make me laugh. That man sleep, eat and breathe you. The mere mention of your name and he jumps to attention. You two living the marshmallow world dream that normal people only read about or see in their dreams. Now mirages, this shit right here is a mirage. You lying on this table playing your own damn doctor is a mirage if I ever seen one. Hold on."

"Is something wrong?"

"The neurobot is set on human mode so I can't get a reading on the cyborg chip. Uhuh. There's no medication in the chambers nor the reserves. Bone dry. Looks like it ran out months ago. When was the last time you got it refilled?"

"No one told me it needed to be refilled."

"Annually. Reminders are sent through Lifeware. Dr. Armsby's medicbot takes care of that for all his patients. Takes five minutes. That little knob at the base of your skull, that's what it's for. The medicbot injects the medicine there to refill the chambers. It has to be removed."

"Can you do it?"

"What, the removal?"

"If it stays in, it'll fry my brain and I'll have no choice but become a full cyborg. If I take it out, I'll have no support system to handle what life throws at me. What if I'm no longer me? What if the way I feel about Xavier is not real? I don't want to be out there alone, V."

"Bitch you've been doing it on your own for months already with no help. That was all you. The mesh has to be removed. I wish I could help but this here neurobot will blast everything I do to the medical board like a ninny at a church picnic. They'll have questions, I won't lie and I can't lose my job. They want each patient to go through the prescribed channels as PHAC has eyes and ears everywhere. One mistake and they'll shut us down for not playing by their rules, especially to avert this cranial mesh medical crisis. You know I'd do anything to help. "

"What am I supposed to do, V?"

"Make an appointment and ask for me. I'm booked through next month but could squeeze you in a few days."

"Days?"

"Yeah, girl.   The augmentation market is hot. Either that or contact the PHAC.   They'll make sure you're seen at the earliest."

"Fuck the PHAC. Once I present myself to them, I've pretty much consented to be fucked with and bombarded with notifications to augment some other body part. They'll never stop until I've surrendered my whole being and to add insult to injury, they let anybody have access to people's medical information."

"It's only a matter of time anyway. Girl, that's one battle we can't win. Might as well suck it up."

"I'm not giving in to the PHAC."

"Just don't do anything stupid. They'll get what they want eventually. Make the appointment. "

"Since you can't or won't help, I better go."

"We coming over for drinks soon, right?"

"Yeah, soon. Talk to you."

"Crazy ass bitch."

10 DISCOVERY

They said the results from the blackout would be back in a few days and in the meantime prescribed rest. The wait is brutal.

The memory of Dr. Armsby office makes me squirm. I'm so embarrassed. I don't know how I'll ever face V again.

"Can I get you anything? Coffee, water, a foot rub?"

Tom's look of concern makes me smile to know I'm well taken care of. His Bay mode is a gentler personality. Xavier seems less tense around him and less possessive. I hate the way he seems distracted lately.

"No thanks, Tom. Shelly might do with a foot rub though," he says, busily navigating a holographic screen, stopping for seconds to peruse the content before moving on to the next screen.

"I'm fine. What are you researching, X?"

I sit up and my back aches a little from reclining on the sofa for what seems like hours. I search his face for a clue to tell me something, anything—are we okay; is he; have I been unbearable with no emotional rescue from my cranial mesh; did I forget to do something; is it a good time to have the talk—the new talk families now have when one of them must decide to relinquish their humanness?

"I can't keep this from her any longer," Xavier says, dragging the holograph to where I'm sitting.

"What's going on?"

Tom approaches Xavier and I'm beginning to like it better when they were suspicious of each other and not as friendly towards one another. Talking behind my back is uncomfortable even knowing they would do anything for me.

"This."

Xavier pulls up an interactive graph with dots joined by a line at certain intervals.

"It shows those moments when you're having an episode," Tom explains. "They're happening more frequent."

"How would you even know when I was having one of 'those' moments if I didn't tell you?"

"Your respiratory index increases and so does your blood pressure. I'm able to track your basal health anywhere and anytime. Your last moment occurred at

6:45 this morning, right when you awoke. Didn't you notice any physical changes at all?"

I shake my head still processing the fact they've joined up together and are keeping secrets from me, even if it is to help.

"Maybe you should send this data to your physicians. I can add it to your medical record."

"That won't be necessary, Tom. It would mean more tests and prodding. It'll pass, just like everything else, with rest."

"Alright, if you think it's nothing. We'll keep looking."

11 RESEARCH

Staying focused is so difficult when you're expecting at any moment something weird could happen to you. I'm looking for it. Waiting for it. Xavier softly snores beside me. I look at him sleeping comfortably while I toss and turn wondering if tea or coffee will relax or make me more tense. The temperature is uncomfortably hot so I kick off the blanket, slide on my slippers and head downstairs.

"Hey, Shelly."

Tom never sleeps and that means I always have company whether I want it or not.

"Hey. Think I'll get a glass of water."

"I was waiting until morning to tell you about my research."

"Yes, go on."

"First, a cross reference of the machine name from the device I couldn't sync with came up as a neuromedical device made a few years ago by Praxis Neurochemicals. It would mean a human in the vicinity has the device installed."

"It's probably an error."

"I certainly hope so. The device also appears on a recall list for it was recently updated with a software upgrade meant for cyborgs. It's certain death for a human if the device is not promptly removed."

"You certainly have a way with words. Does Xavier know this?"

"I haven't mentioned it."

"Keep it between us. Understood?"

"Understood."

"What else did you find?"

"A report from the scientific community tracks and monitors spatial events and one of them mentioned a recent spike in radiological spurts across the solar system."

"And?"

I didn't mean to but a little chuckle escaped my lips.

"And, the spurts match in frequency the moments you've had."

"That's coincidence. You're trying too hard to find a reason, Tom.   If radiological spurts had an effect on me, I'm sure it would also affect others. Blogs and online postings of people claiming unusual changes in their health would trend. Then it would reach the main media channels and we would have already heard of it."

"I see your point. Only thing is, I don't have access to social media to check."

"After Kirk it was a design decision to not allow ComBorg's to be influenced by unmonitored and unsupervised forums. All IxTar employees are banned from social media, so I'm afraid I can't help you either."

"How about Xavier?"

"You two are besties now. Ask him to take a look when he wakes."

It came out in the wrong tone.

"Good night, Shelly."

He leaves the kitchen. I place the glass on the sink without taking a sip.

My hand reaches for the tiny knob on the base of my skull where the cranial mesh terminates. My head pounds. I get the urge to rip it off my head.

12 CORRELATION

"Wake up, sleepy head."

I open my eyes, grateful to see another day. Xavier hovers over me with a greasy bag. The smell of grilled cheese makes my stomach growl.

"Morning. Where'd you find grilled cheese at this hour?" I ask, stretching to get the kinks out.

"It's lunch time, babe."

I jump up to a sitting position and look around for my Pulsometer to check the time. I didn't have anywhere to be but still it's not like me to sleep in even on the weekend. He kisses my forehead.

"What are you doing home so early?"

"Where's your head? It's Sunday. I've rescheduled Santa Fe for next weekend. You don't mind?"

"No worries."

"Tom said you gave him homework last night."

"What did he tell you?"

"Calm down. You're acting like he told me you've asked him to check up on me or something."

Blood rushes to my cheeks and I force myself to act natural.

"I told him to ask you to look into social media to see if anyone is posting topics on sporadic fevers and visual disturbances that might coincide with radiological spurts," I say.

I take the bag from him and pull the sandwich.

"And, that's what I spent the better part of the morning doing. So, like I told Tom, there were some posts, but not high enough in numbers to trend. Valerie, Gina and Mandy look into the poster's profiles and their online history to assess whether what they were posting could be trusted or if they were trolls, or just weird."

It's like I hadn't eaten in days. I licked the cheese from my fingers.

"And?"

He looks at me and makes a face. *What? I was hungry.* I crumble the greasy wrapper and hand it to him.

"Most of them checked out. I guess whatever it is you're experiencing is not so uncommon. I asked them to send us the data aggregation and we should get it any minute now to plot against the spurts. It should make you feel at ease but most of them brushed it off like it's nothing."

"So, I'm a delusional crybaby," I snap back.

Mr. Nardini flashes across my mind. Could he have been overly sensitive to specific stimuli why he became a mind-tampering victim?

"Calm yourself," he says.

Telling me to calm down only confirms I'm not calm and starts a snowball effect. Whatever is happening is making my world seem glitchy.

Xavier's Pulsometer beeps.

My heart jumps wondering if it's the next of kin notification the neurobot sent. Hopefully his filter is set to send them to the spam folder. He swipes the virtual screen. It converts into a holographic representation of a speckled multicolored line graph. A large blotch is located at 6:45AM yesterday with singular dots along the rest of the time line.

"What is that multicolored blotch?"

"A cluster. Let me get Tom to take a look."

"Hold on. Not in our private bedroom, remember? I'll meet you both in the kitchen in five."

"Bossy, bossy."

He thinks I'm the bossy one?

"Allow me to put claim to the little privacy I have left," I say.

"Hurry up, babe."

Five minutes later with brushed teeth and washed face, I slip on my satin robe and head downstairs. The two are chatting like buddies in front of a new holographic line graph.

I look at the chart to see what the fuss is about but it needs explaining.

"What are you two gossiping about?"

"My office sent us more data from the social media forums going back the past month. See anything interesting yet?"

I know that tone. It's something he wants me to discover for myself. I focus, zooming in on the lines and corresponding datapoints.   There are now three separate lines on the graph. One labeled 'Shelly', the other "Posters" and the last one "Disturbances".

"What's the "Disturbances"?

"That's data mined from the Oracabessa Interstellar Events report," Tom says. "For every event this past week, you've had a corresponding moment. Look at 6:45 yesterday."

"Ok. Several observatories reported an interstellar disturbance right around the time of my moment. The posts from the forums also saw a spike around that time. These posts don't mention fever. They had sporadic glitches in their communication devices. Back to square one."

"Well, hold on. The Bison Observatory reported its highest ever EMP," Xavier says, reading another holograph.

"The frequency of these spikes are unusual," says Tom.

Xavier holds out his arms for me to join him. He pulls me closer.

"Babe, EMPs could have an effect on your cranial mesh. I think it's time you remove it. You're over the incident, right?" he whispers.

"Right."

Xavier's Pulsometer beeps.

But would I ever get over losing you? Losing myself?

I scoot off his lap onto the other end of the sofa. He swipes out the message. It displays in a holograph.

"They're working today?" I ask.

"I told them their jobs depended on it."

"You're kidding, right?"

"Of course. But you should have seen your face."

"Anything?"

"The 6:45 was probably a fluke..."

It lasts for a second, like the frame in a movie, but the image is clear and seems to span a minute or longer because of the detail. My heart skips a beat and a sensation covers me and in this moment a feeling sears through me like this discussion has happened before. We are all there in the same clothes, same temperament in the brief moving image. The three of us, just as we are now, our words and movements become an exact replay.

I watch as the blip pass and the disjointed return to real life—Xavier shifts his weight looking at the hologram and Tom turns his head to look at me.

"She just had another one," Tom says, busily checking on a separate hologram.

Xavier hurries to my side. "You alright, babe?"

I'm shell-shocked replaying the moment in my mind. *I did just see that,* I tell myself, just in case the memory dissipates.

I nod in response. They appear busy, knee deep in solving my problem while I sit helpless. What if they're mistaken and chasing the wrong lead?

"They won't report the event if there's one for hours. I need direct access to their telescope database and monitoring tools," Tom says.

"Try an international observatory. Some allow public access," Xavier says. "Wait, is it safe for him to traverse international sites?"

"He has to go through the approved IxTar servers and they'll allow it as long as it's an approved research domain," I say.

Xavier's Pulsometer beeps and all eyes are on him. He swipes the new social media report onto the holograph. A larger blotch than 6:45 yesterday appears at 11:30AM—only minutes ago of social media reports related to sporadic communication outages.

Xavier and I gather closer to the holograph to examine and analyze the updated graph showing event clusters. Tom appears distracted. He adds a new line graph to the holograph darkening the new blotched area.

"What's that?" Xavier asks.

"Correlation," Tom answers.

13 DECODE

With the observatory reports coinciding with my 11:30 coming in from observatories all over the world, Tom's new line graph validates his theory.

"You're so stubborn. What more do you need to see what's happening?" Xavier says.

"We need Shelly to have another one of her moments. Three in a row, then I think she'll believe. I'll do more research in the meantime."

"It's not something I can conjure, y'know."

Tom slips away and leaves the room. I think he wants to give us space. It's a behavior he's been programmed to recognize to give us enough room without him so his presence doesn't become bothersome or overwhelming.

"Whether the mesh is causing these headaches, sudden onset fevers and memory lapses, you don't need it. They are susceptible to bugs."

"They don't know. IxTar doesn't know. I could lose my job if they know I have this cranial mesh to cope with past trauma. They rely on my ability to be objective but many see a cranial mesh as a handicap or the next logical step before transitioning to a cyborg. My job is specifically for a human, not a broken one or one on the edge of becoming a machine. I don't trust Dr. Armsby or the facility with my privacy."

"Hmm. Armsby. I knew that name sounded familiar. His practice was breached."

"Every patient he sees he's forced to report their medical information to the PHAC. X, what if they find something that can be fixed by augmentation? I'd have no choice but to comply or become an Outlier. I could lose everything."

"I know people, babe. You don't have to use the public system or Armsby. Let's get it removed, then we'll force PHAC to amend the medical information they have on you. We'll tell them it's a mistake, a stolen identity. They won't have a reason to come after you. I don't know what else you want me to say. It's a good plan but it's your choice if you want to live with something that's messing with your life that can be easily remedied. I just want my woman back."

What if the real me is too much for you? What if you hurt me, Xavier? What if this world has evolved so much that it's not suitable for people who are sensitive, like me? What if the PHAC insist on verifying what we tell them, or find out we've lied or their test leads to some other augmentation? Will you still want me?

He hugs me tight. He doesn't see the holes in his plan but I do. He hasn't given me any real reason to distrust him but for some reason I'm looking for it, the warning signs, like a dog waiting for its master. It's almost like I'll be relieved if he's dishonest and my mistrust is likely to push him away. I can't stop the thoughts, the feelings, waiting for the gut punch.

"You're going in?" I ask, pulling away. I'm sure he has other important things to do than babysit his potentially crazy girlfriend. I'd gotten use to him disappearing for a few hours to work in the quiet stillness of his empty office on some weekends.

"You want me to?"

His facial expression is neutral. I think he's doing it on purpose to not influence my decision.

"Yes, Tom and I need our alone time."

He makes a face.

"Then I'm staying," he says. A smile crosses his lips as he reaches over to put his arms around me again.

"You better," I say, glad he made the decision I hoped he'd make. My insecurities fade. I squeeze him tight.

"Babe, I didn't want to say this in front of Tom but we need to be careful what we put in the trash. Remember, everything is a datapoint, even a used tissue has DNA and is traceable back to us. My team had to reach out to a website to remove our data."

"Those bastards Shamewared us?   That's disgusting and embarrassing.   Remember how it started?"

"A recycling program to help us sort our trash correctly, then expanded to show us how we were being wasteful then expanded to communicate with our grocery app to let it know when we're running low or running out of an item."

"And now? Still think we ought to slip out the old and slip in the new? Are we to burn our trash to preserve our dignity and privacy?"

"It's one battle we've already lost. On the bright side it's effective against overflowing landfills and littering. But an incinerator or autoclave might not be a bad idea otherwise we have to accept whatever is thrown out is no longer ours and is traceable."

Ugh.

Slipping out the house has taken more effort and time than planned. The sun hovers above the horizon beating the streets to make humans take protective cover. The area fills with aerial and land patrollers causing the streets to be temporarily emptied. Even offline they pick up Carisa's registration noting any extended time spent in this part of town. They'll check to see if Carisa's computer was disabled so it could be stolen.

A hobo rummages through a nearby trash can with both hands. He kicks the drum finding nothing he wants. His bloodshot eyes roam the vicinity and lands on Carisa parked nearby. Cautiously he approaches the vehicle admiring the sleek finish. With Carisa offline I'm a sitting duck with none of the protections enabled to save the occupants in case of an accident, rough terrain or vandalism. He hasn't spotted me yet. I look around to see if she's here. This is the same spot I'd dropped her a couple days ago. The hobo kicks Carisa. I bite the bullet and press the online button. Carisa's internal and external lights illuminate.

"Engage protective mode."

Carisa's gentle hum stuns the man. He takes a step back, then circles the vehicle looking for a way in. His tattered dirt stained clothes cling to his body. He picks up a piece of trash and hurls it at the car.

"Tooman!"

That's the name the Outliers have given us, the humans who are in between the extremes, the two-faced humans.

The click of the doors being locked and the external door handles merging into the sides is a welcomed comfort. Other hobos and Outliers emerge from their hidden places and begin their curious approach as the hobo screams angrily. The bulletproof window panes descend from their compartment to cover all glass panes adding a darkened tint so the occupants could see out but no one sees in.

"Protective mode engaged. Should I take extended safety measures?"

"Not necessary. Let's head up the street."

One of the many parklets the city had installed a few years ago come into view. With the throng behind us, I wonder if she's here.

"Let me out."

Carisa obeys disengaging the protective mode and releasing the lock on the door to open it.

Trash is everywhere. Buildings that were once pristine are scourged with graffiti. Landscape that was once green and plentiful have branches hang limp from dehydration. Drones buzz overhead. One breaks formation and stops a few feet away at eye level. Without saying anything it flies away and rejoins its group. Carisa follows as I walk along the walkway, cross it and enter another parklet where I'd spot movement. A woman and young child sit on one of the benches eating what appears to be a leftover sandwich. Their eyes follow me, the older woman's with scorn.

"Mom, a tooman."

"Disgusting. Shame on you!"

I keep walking to get to the figure standing up against a statue at the end of the tiny park. The man adjusts his clothes while a stream of yellow liquid run from the statue out onto the walkway.

"What're you doing down here, tooman?   It's unsafe to be walking these streets alone."

He smiles to reveal yellowed and missing teeth as he wipes his hand in his clothes.

I gasp and look around for Carisa but I'm too far from the road.

What the heck am I doing here?

He stamps his foot and waves his arms in the air. I spot Carisa way on the other side of the road. With all my might I run towards the car. His laughter mocks me. I stop in mid-step, turn around and approach him. The look of terror on his face give me the jolt of confidence I need.

"I'm looking for someone."

"I bet no one here is looking for you."

"Brunette with dark freckles, late thirties, about five feet six inches, six to eight months pregnant. I dropped her down the street from here a couple days ago. She was wearing a brown coat with a green scarf."

"That narrows it down. What'd you want with her?"

"Have you seen a woman matching that description?"

"What's your business with her? You family?"

"Look. I need to find her before it gets dark. You said yourself it gets dangerous at night. Just tell me if you know an Outlier who attended the protest on the bridge a couple days ago matching her description. I'm not here to get her in trouble."

"One, maybe two hundred such who'd fit that description but only a handful brave enough to show their faces. Check the park across the street."

"Thanks."

"That's it?"

I thought of the crumpled dollar the woman had thrown on the car seat and how unprepared I am to be in this part of town that values anonymity.

"Sorry. I do think your cause is a noble one. It takes a lot of heart to say no to what comes easy."

"Just as much guts as it takes to be in this part of town. Good luck."

Carisa hovers on the closest street following and waiting for me. Solar streetlights pop on and off fooled by the temporary darkness of wavering tall trees. The parklet's interior is dark but as I approach the air is thick with whispers. I step around the overturned garbage scaring birds pecking at the refuse. Their faces come into view like light bulbs.

"It's a tooman."

"Here?"

"Must be lost."

"What does she want?"

I approach the group. They stand as I get closer.

"Hi. Sorry to bother you. I'm looking for a woman I gave a lift a few days ago. I dropped her off a few blocks that way. Brunette, pregnant, feisty. She gave me something," I say, holding the crumpled dollar bill in my hand. "Something I need to return."

They look at each other and made faces.

"Wasn't none of us."

The crunch of a twig behind them made them look. A shadow slowly walks forward. I take a step back. The shadow steps into the sun's moody glow. Freckled brunette wearing a brown coat and green scarf looks at me with sad brown eyes. I had forgotten that feature. Her middle protrudes even more noticeable than before. Definitely closer to eight or nine months.

"Simone," one of them whisper.

She glares at the woman who said her name then stares at me with curiosity. I stare back thinking of my luck having found her. The others step aside to let her through as she approaches me.

"The proper response is thanks. Not to be looking for me all over the city to give me back what I gave you. Too good for my money?"

"It's not that. Not that at all. A friend was helping out a friend."

"We're not friends."

"As you wish," I say, holding out the dollar bill. "Can I speak to you privately for a minute?"

She steps pass me ignoring the relic and head to a secluded part of the parklet closer to the street. Carisa stops nearby.

"Speak."

"I don't know how to say this so I'll come straight to the point. You're due soon, how will you deliver the baby?"

"What is that any business of yours?" she says angrily.

"What I mean is, your midwife, doctor or caregiver, they're black market, right?"

"And?"

"I need a name, for a friend who needs to have a procedure. A name and address to…"

"What's wrong with you? No one goes there unless they're in hiding or desperate."

"Please…"

She snatches the crumpled dollar from my hand.

"8668 Willow Street. Entrance in back. They're open 24/7."

"A name?"

"Doctor whoever you want them to be. I gotta go."

"Thanks."

"Call it even."

"The girls are coming over for a ladies' night. You won't mind?"

It had been a while since my 'girls' Felicia, Georgina, Viola, Sam and I got together. I need some girl bonding and to set things right with V.

"Not at all. Just have Tom run the descaler when they leave. You never know who'll bring those little nasty nanodrones with them; turn our home into a live entertainment hub at the pleasure of lowlifes who have nothing better to do. Think I'll head down to McKurdles for a drink now that my team has wiped our social media searches from our servers," he says. "Wish the robot could come."

"He's not just any old tin can robot. Why do you keep saying that? How would you like it if he referred to us as 'the humans'?"

"He does it to get me to defend myself, my existence and my programming," Tom says, entering the room on cue.

"And it works, doesn't it? Listen, I want you to keep an eye on our patient. If she has another one of those moments, contact me immediately."

He stands and I scoot back into the sofa claiming his spot so I could stretch out and enjoy what's left of his warmth.

"Will do. We better get ready for the ladies," Tom says, bringing up a hologram with a shopping list and a bunch of other to-dos. "Oh dear, we're running low on tequila and gin. I'll have some delivered immediately."

"Tom, a word."

They leave me on the sofa to go to the kitchen. I know they're talking about me.

A beep sounds from my Pulsometer. A representative from PHAC appears in a hologram before I could deny the intrusion.

"This message is for Shelly Greene. After numerous failed attempts to obtain your cooperation, the Public Health Advisory Council has issued a medical warrant to forcibly remove your installed cranial mesh. Your location has been successfully determined and a permanent satellite link has been established with your device for tracking purposes. You have 12 hours to surrender to your local PHAC office on your own accord or be arrested for ignoring a health warning and breach of the public trust. Any effort by you to cross state lines or leave the country will be construed as an act of aggression."

I press the delete button, but the hologram fails to delete.

"Delete message," I say.

"Receipt confirmation is required."

I feel trapped. Forced. How else can I get rid of an insistent hologram?

I glance towards the kitchen and the two are finishing their secret tete-a-tete. This is something they cannot know.

"Message received," I say. This is how it starts— how I lose my free will.

"Thank you. A reminder will be sent in three-hour increments."

My speeding heart rate will catch Tom's attention. *Relax.* Xavier kisses my forehead.

"Alright, see you two later, and don't overdo it. I'd like to have company when I return."

He flashes a smile that I wonder if I'd ever see again, if I would appreciate it as a cyborg at best, or worse.

"Hurry back," I said, pulling the throw over my legs.

"Have fun."

He opens the door and closes it behind him. Chills run the length of my body. I pull the blanket up under my chin to calm the shivers. I inhale deeply. It smells like Xavier.

"Shelly?"

Did we have everything? My mind keeps reverting to Xavier and Tom's secret discussion then travels off to the meeting with the Outlier woman dressed in every piece of clothes she owns.   Food, drink and entertainment, that's what I need to focus on. I put them out of my mind and I'm stuck on entertainment. What could we do for entertainment? I'll leave it up to them to decide when they get here.

"Shelly?"

"Not now, Tom. I'll be right back."

Not having seen Willow street, I had no option but to have Carisa navigate.

"ETA 10 minutes."

The building is an abandoned hospital on a secluded road with trailers and discarded rusting old gas guzzlers parked all around it. A partly demolished wing scaffolding careens and swing wildly to dissuade anyone from entering. The giant placard with the hospital's name is overgrown with weeds making the only letters 'pit' visible.

A man with a bandaged head is being helped to a park car by a man in a white lab coat. He waves and drives off. The other man returns to the back of the building.

This time I came prepared. Twenty crisp hundred-dollar bills are stashed in my purse. There's more, if necessary. I remove my Pulsometer and leave it on the seat.

"Carisa, after I leave, please engage protective mode."

"Protective mode pending."

"Thanks. I'll be right back. Don't leave until I return."

Carisa opens the door and I step out. If I analyze this, it'll just confirm this is a bad idea.

Another patient is escorted by another man in a stained white lab coat. I pass them to hurry to the entrance.

I turn the doorknob. The dimly lit room with flickering lights and water rhythmically dripping from the partially collapsed ceiling into awaiting buckets catches my attention that's then stolen by a whiff of something powerful to cover up an even more offensive odor. The ten or so chairs are filled with people in distressed situations. Some moan, others cough, a baby or two cries out. A woman dressed in a blue hospital gown sits behind a desk where a brighter light shone on a sign to sign in here. I hadn't seen pens and white writing paper since I was a child. I scribbled the name, Simone.

Screams from a room in the back startles me. Everyone else appear unfazed by the outburst. A man in a white lab coat burst from the room.

"We're gonna need another one of those. Quick!" he says, before running back to the room.

The receptionist jumps to her feet and rushes into the room.

The screams grow louder and louder, then suddenly quiet.

I wait for new screams, more screams from the same man, but nothing.

A few minutes later, the sound of a siren gets louder and stops right outside the building. Two emergency medical practitioners wheel a gurney into the entrance. The Receptionist emerges blood splattered and direct the men into the room. A minute later, the gurney is wheeled out, slid into the back of the ambulance. It takes off with the siren on full blast.

A woman in the waiting room grabs her child's hand and dash out the door.

"Who's next?" a man says out loud to no one in particular. "Those cranial mesh are tricky. They say the adjustment afterwards is a real bitch."

The Receptionist emerges removing her soiled lab coat, throwing it in the trash and putting on another. She leans over the sign-in tab while rubbing her hands in a blue gel.

"Gorey Sadman."

She looks out onto the remaining patients waiting to be seen. No one budge. The man who spoke suddenly jumps to his feet.

"That'd be me."

"All cash, understood," says the Receptionist.

"Just get it out."

"You here with someone?"

"Just me."

"Right this way."

The receptionist takes him into a room across from the one the last patient was seen.

"Dr. Bearer will be right with you."

A new patient enters and sign in taking Gorey's vacated chair. She sidles up to me.

"Who they have in today, Peter or Paul?"

A piercing scream fills the air. Peeling paint falls from the walls splashing brown water from a bucket onto the floor, covering my shoe.

I glance at her wondering how she'd know the doctors and be so familiar to call them by their first names.

"Hmm. Yep. It's Paul. At least his patients scream. I use to work here," she says. "Just back to collect my last paycheck. They've made some improvements with the place."

She looks around, nodding, before settling down.

Another scream jolts me.

The woman leans in and says conspiratorially, "I got something that'll take the edge off. Twenty a pop. They'll charge fifty."

Screams in succession grow louder and louder.

The room door flies open.

"Debra, we need another. Hurry!" he says, before running back to the room.

The receptionist slams the book she was reading onto the desk and jumps to her feet. She makes a call and rush into the room.

More screams follow.

The sound of the approaching ambulance is déjà vu. In a few minutes, Gorey is wheeled out, screaming at the top of his lungs.

The receptionist returns to the desk and changes her blood splattered gown.

"Simone."

"Simone."

I take a detour to head downtown. The parklet where I'd found the Outlier woman comes into view.

"Let me out here, Carisa. I'll be a moment."

The same group of people and others I hadn't seen before are there. They stare with an equal amount of disgust and awe.

"She's back. The tooman is back," a woman says.

"Simone, your friend is here," says another.

Simone waddles out and stops, then approach me.

"What now? Looking for a place to stay?"

"This is for you. If you need more, or a place to stay, this is my address."

I hand her the cash and return to Carisa without looking back.

"Let's go home, Carisa."

"What were you doing in the Hallows?   Did something happen to you?"

Tom looks me over with that look I've come to know as care but I want to be left alone.

"What is it, Tom?"

I'm exhausted. Defeated. There's nothing else I can do but give in.

"Remember I mentioned earlier the disturbances the observatory reported were major?"

"Yup."

"Those major wavelengths are followed by minor ones."

"And?"

"I isolated the minor wavelengths after each major and ..."

I wait for him to continue though he doesn't usually pause mid-sentence. I look at him to see if he's glitching out but he seems deep in thought.

"And?"

"Interesting. I just got some more data. The minor wavelengths from these disturbances all match. The major ones vary in length and intensity but the ones that follow are always the same. It's almost like a signature."

"You think there's meaning to the data and not a random EMP?"

"I'll extract the minor wavelengths and run them against my QPU. Oh, excuse me the delivery is here."

He walks to the door and opens it before the bell rings. The delivery drone hovers, recognizing and validating an adult over 21 is home. It opens its storage compartment to reveal a neatly packed box. Tom reaches in and removes it.

"Thank you and have a good rest of your day," he says before closing the door.

"Did they bring everything you ordered?" I asked.

"Two bottles of tequila, two bottles of spiced gin and one large dry vermouth."

"Is that enough for all of us?"

"We can always order more, if necessary. Did you already pick something out to wear? If not, I suggest the green jumper. It's flattering on you and compliments your eyes."

"Fine, I'll go freshen up."

"Wait."

"Make it quick."

"Each spurt is terminated with the same number sequence. 16, 15, 12, 12, 9, 14, 15, 22, 1."

"What's a spurt?"

"An isolated EMP will have a combination of a major and minor wavelength. The major ones are the burst that's followed by minor ones. This pattern is called a spurt.   Think of it like someone is trying to send a message where the major burst is the envelope that's the vehicle for the minor ones to travel protected because they hold the message. The vehicle withstands all atmospheric and spatial interferences to ensure the passengers arrive safe."

"So, the message would be prized cargo."

"And each envelope tagged with a unique identifier to ensure the vehicle reaches its intended destination. They're encoded with a specific encryption key that is used to decode the message. I've ran these keys across all the deviations I know and encryption algorithms in our databank, but zero match. Maybe it's not that sophisticated or we're way off. I've tried coordinates, international phone numbers, communication frequencies..."

I zone out when the sound of my favorite gameshow catches my attention.

"When the saints go marching."

"What?" Tom says.

"The answer to the puzzle."'

It's one of the very few televised programs I watch on holovision that's not overstimulating. It's addictive, but in a good way.

"It's missing the vowels," Tom says, shifting his train of thought to watch.

"Buy an 'E'," I say to the holovision.

"Her chances of solving the puzzle would increase significantly if she bought an 'A'."

Tom's suggestion is droned out as I watch the contestant take a moment to decide her next move.

"I'd like to buy an 'I'."

Ding. Ding. Ding. The audience applauds.

"There are two 'Is'. Would you like to solve or spin?" the game host says.

"That was the second-best option," Tom says, walking away and heading towards the kitchen.

I turn the volume down to give Tom my attention then glance at the hologram and the winner of the round had previously requested the vowel 'E'. All that's left to do is read the words to solve the puzzle and claim the prize.

"When the saints go marching," she says.

"Took you long enough," I said.

An alarm outside blares.

Beeps sound from my Pulsometer. Not again. A protective officer hologram appears in the family room.

"This is a public announcement for your region. Due to extreme weather and energy fluctuation and for your protection, please stay indoors, lock your doors and windows and reduce energy consumption. Your compliance is required. This is an announcement from the Energy Conservatorship. "

I breathe a sigh of relief. The heat index has risen to 120 degrees. There's an ongoing water shortage, protests are getting more violent and homes are being looted.

Tom enters the living room. He's muttering.

"I need more data to find suitable patterns. The accuracy of these predictions is very low."

The next round of the game show starts. It's a long puzzle and all the lighted squares are blank. I have to consciously force myself to look away. Checking each window around the house to ensure they're locked is the distraction I need. It's also the perfect excuse to see what's happening outside.

An ambulance is parked in Mr. Nardini's driveway. A body lies on a stretcher, covered with a white sheet. The head enclosed in a hyperbaric helmet.   Tom approaches.

"His cranial mesh erupted.   Now he'll be a full cyborg. Must have been his cranial mesh I detected all along. I'll have my proximity sensors calibrated."

I look away to push the thought from my mind. Did they give him 12 hours to turn himself in? Did the device erupt on its own? Was it another hacking or tampering attempt?

"Are any of those numbers on the tail greater than 26?"

"Twenty-two is the highest," he says.

"Try the alphabet.   Make each number in the sequence correspond to a letter."

Before I'm done, he stands and looks at me blankly like he's calculating a math problem.

"P-O-L-L-I-N-O-V-A. Pollinova."

He looks at me, eyes unblinking.

"Is that a thing?"

"I've found a super observatory in Utah."

"Can you get into their databanks? Maybe it's their deep space EMP that's ricocheting back to earth."

It's another dead end, or coincidence. Why would EMPs have anything to do with a bad software upgrade, the mirages and sudden onset fevers? There's nothing solid to go on. It's time to let Xavier in on the part I left out and report to the PHAC office first thing in the morning.

"Why don't you get dressed? Your guests will arrive in an hour. Shelly?"

It's a moment. I try to prolong it and memorize everything I see in the last still frame: I'm standing in the center of a huge hollow concrete enclosure open to the skies. The middle is concave while the ends are flared. A cold gust of wind swirl and echoes through the chamber as it whips my hair, dampens my cheeks. The scene disintegrates. I've never been there or seen anything like it though there's a sense of familiarity.

"I just had another."

"I know. The EMP is not originating from the observatory."

"How do you know?"

"I'm in their system right now. The message they send is 'greetings, from earth'. This electromagnetic pulse came from outside our solar system and has no attached message."

"But why would it say Pollinova?"

Tom initiates a new hologram showing the outside of the Pollinova Super X-ray Observatory. The huge cinched cylindrical structure is situated on top of a mountain and looks like a storage unit for cement. He touches a virtual tour button and it zooms to show the inside of the structure. I gasp.

"That's the place I just saw in the moment. What else can you find out?"

"The good stuff is highly secured and only accessible to their research personnel."

"I have to see it in person."

"We can plan a trip for this weekend with Xavier when the emergency lifts. I'll make the arrangements."

"I can't wait. I have to know what this is."

"Shelly, the medic advised rest. Utah is hours away. By the time we get there they'll be closed. And we're in a state-wide emergency."

I head to the coat closet and drag a light jacket off a hanger. It ricochets off the rack and bounce to the floor. I grab my purse and change my shoes to a comfortable pair I slip on. Tom's shoes are on the closet floor beside Xavier's. I throw them in his direction.

"You coming?"

He quickly slips them on and is on my heel as I head to the door. "I promised to let Xavier know if you had another one of those 'episodes'."

"Don't. You. Dare."

I stare at him with venom to let him know I mean it.   He's stunned and unresponsive.   His control mechanism kicks in as his system reboots.   I had yet to test this feature of the CB-X in addition to the safe word that when said shuts it down.   One minute has never lasted this long.

"Hello, Shelly.   How are you?"

"Awesome.   We're   due   at   the   Pollinova Observatory."

14 POLLINOVA

"Your guests are arriving. Shall I let them in?"

They must think I'm the worse friend in the world, always asking for forgiveness. How can I explain I had to leave and run an errand to preserve my emotional sanity and my humanity? Once again things are happening around me and I can't simply ignore them and go on like they're not there. It's like I'm compelled to solve the puzzle and I won't rest until I do. This, I know for sure is my last shot.

"Send them a message I've been delayed and to make themselves at home. Purchase two first class tickets on the next express jet to Ogden. Where is Xavier?"

"I've located him at McKurdle's in the company of Jack Cunningham and Sarah Sommersby. His respiratory functions are within normal limits."

"Anything else, Tom?"

"Mr. Cunningham and Ms. Sommersby are not."

"Are not what?"

"I believe the common term is they are 'plastered'."

"For heaven's sake. I thought they made it so other people's privacy would be respected."

"My apologies. The module is optional. I can have it disengaged, if you'd wish."

"Would you still be able to monitor Xavier?"

"I would not."

"Never mind then. How much longer until we're there?"

"Based on current speeds and rush hour traffic, 20-minutes."

"Carisa, find a detour. I need the quickest route."

"Checking all possible routes. You are on the fastest route to SFO."

"Tom, did you check the last spurts to see if they were the same?"

"I'll do that now. Just received a notification our tickets were declined."

"Why?"

"Travel across state lines is discouraged unless it's official business or a personal emergency that must be justified."

Yeah, right.

"Try using the IxTar expense account."

"That worked. Checking on the spurts."

"I should have grabbed something to eat.   I'm starving," I said.

"Shall I make a way-stop at a local restaurant?" Carisa says.

"No, I'll get something at the airport or on the plane. Just keep checking for the fastest route. Tom, when does the flight leave?"

"The last direct flight leaves at 5:10."

"How long is it?"

"Forty minutes, depending on tailwinds."

"Have a car ready for us when we land. Something rugged that can take the mountains."

"Working on it."

"What time does the observatory close?"

"The observation deck and telescopes are open twenty-four seven."

"Yes, for visitors.   What we need is behind the counter, in the backrooms, under lock and key."

"What are you suggesting?"

"Nothing for you to worry about. Let me see a map of the facility again."

He launches a hologram of the Pollinova Observatory. I take over the image and widen it to get a better view of the outsides and entrance. Goosebumps cover my skin and a chill run along my spine. The uncanny resemblance to the image I had seen about an hour again stirs an urge to get there quickly. What does all this mean? My mind is busy trying to fill in the blanks and I've never felt more impatient and alive. I rotate a little too far to one side and another building is located nearby. It's a single story dwarfed in comparison to the observatory.

"Hold on, what's that?" I say.

Tom inches closer on the seat to get a better look. He touches the pixelated image lightly and a caption pops up.

"MemServ Data Center."

"Figures they'd need a way to conveniently store all the data they capture non-stop."

"That's a private company. They specialize in storing memory uploads. Law enforcement and the health system mine the uploaded data to evaluate the mind health of cyborgs, predict criminal behavior and use it as evidence to help solve cases. Xavier uses them."

"For what purpose?"

"To store your memories. After the incident he's taken many precautions."

"That's impossible.   That technology is only for cyborgs."

He's awkwardly quiet.

"What aren't you telling me?"

"Xavier should tell you himself."

"Tell me what?   Now you have boundaries and loyalties to him?   I demand to know what you know, right now."

My voice is firm but not venomous for him to shut down.

"You've arrived.   Your flight is on time and leaving gate N63," Carisa says.   "I'll be on stand-by in the autolot."

Tom is booking.   I want to tell him to slow down but I'm still burning from what he told me.

"We better hurry.   The flight leaves in twenty minutes."

His voice is steady.   Why do I feel I just had an argument with myself?

"This discussion is not over.   Can we go straight to the gate?"

"You have no baggage, so yes."

No baggage.   I seemed to have picked up some on the way here.   Everything has been going extremely well with Xavier. There's no one else I trust in this world but now I feel betrayed and I'm not sure there isn't a good explanation. Why am I being lumped in with addicts, people with neurological disorders, phobias and those who've been reskilled with new capabilities to keep up in the labor market when all I need is a dopamine inhibitor?

We rush along the long winding corridors. Up ahead the terminal comes into view. Overhead the nonstop public announcement fills the quiet.

To ensure public safety, travelers are reminded to ensure they observe all laws of their arrival and destination vicinities...

Popup boutiques, bookstores, restaurants, cosmetics and beauty shops are on both sides of the wide thoroughfare. The middle has automatic walkways to jet passengers to their gates and terminals.

"Ms. Greene, Esoterica is having a special sale on facial moisturizers. May I suggest the new Chamomile and Green tea..."

"No thanks.

"Our duty-free sale ends in 1-hour. Purchase two bottles of tequila, two bottles of spiced gin and get one large dry vermouth free."

"Remove me from all your marketing."

"Good afternoon Ms. Greene, may we interest you in our latest..."

"No. Please go away."

"Ms. Greene..."

"The state is under a mandatory curfew for all residents beginning at 10PM to 5AM."

Tom finally slows while I catch up to him at the gate. He connects to the boarding cyborg to validate our tickets.

"Is your machine lithium powered? It won't be allowed to board."

"It? He isn't. He uses cadmium," I say.

"Thanks. Enjoy your flight," the cyborg attendant says.

We don't speak again until we're seated.

"How is Xavier uploading my memories to MemServ?"

"His company created a special add-on software for your cranial mesh. He confided in me so I could be a better assistant, to look out for bugs. I'm sorry to have violated your privacy."

"What else have you kept from me?"

"If you recall, memory uploads are a required social mandate once a human has transitioned."

"I'm still a human, Tom. My cranial mesh is below the 10% cybernetic threshold so how can my memories be extracted and uploaded like a machine's?"

"Your cranial mesh also has a cyborg chip. Xavier's software tapped into the capability to stream electromagnetic pulses without activating the entire device. The pulses are decoded into memories and stored in the same format and data centers as cyborgs."

"Xavier would never do such a thing. Why? Why would he..."

"He did it to protect you."

The flight attendant's announcement comes over the PA system and the safety demonstration is distracting but I watch the cyborg fasten the air mask to her face. Same as I saw in the flash I had yesterday. I lean closer to Tom in the aisle seat and his eyes are fastened to the cyborg.

"Protect me? How is activating a cyborg chip in a human protecting them? What if he made a mistake? So not only do I have to contend with a bad software update and EMPs, Xavier's made his own changes. How will we ever isolate the problem? And why would I ever need a backup of my memories?" I whispered.

Inside I coax myself to calm down. How dare he. We're going to have words when I get back.

"Maybe, it's not for you."

My arms and legs suddenly weigh a ton. What was he afraid of? I'm in deep thought for the remainder of the flight processing this new information.

The aircraft lands after the brief flight and we make a beeline to the rental kiosk to pick up the car Tom reserved.

"The state of Utah is under a mandatory curfew for all residents beginning at 10PM to 7AM."

"Do you want self-driving mode?"

He stops at the front door to the vehicle and the autocab opens its doors.

"Why not? It knows these roads better than we do."

My Pulsometer beeps. A representative from PHAC appears in a hologram.

"This is a reminder for Shelly Greene. The Public Health Advisory Council has issued a medical warrant to forcibly remove your installed cranial mesh. You have 9

hours to surrender to your local PHAC office on your own accord or be arrested for ignoring a health warning and breach of the public trust. Any effort by you to cross state lines or leave the country will be construed as an act of aggression. The next reminder will be sent in three hours."

I press the accept button to rid myself of the unwanted message. Tom looks on with what must be his shock look.

"Yes, I'm a wanted woman. Let's go."

The autocab opens the rear compartment doors. I slide in. Tom shimmies beside me.

"We have to leave before the curfew," he says.

"I'm aware. Pollinova Observatory, please."

The autocab closes the doors and calculates the destination.

"Good evening, CB010X993. The ETA for Pollinova Observatory is 6:08 PM. Please sit back and allow the seatbelt to adjust. Enjoy the ride."

Tom leans in and attempts to whisper in my ear.

"The autocab has picked up my machine name and has broadcasted it to the local Monitoring Magistrate."

Shit. Advanced machines in this state actively monitor individual's whereabouts in public spaces and rentals. Tom is not registered here. They won't stop until he's identified.

The autocab pulls out from the curb and slowly heads out the airport exit.

"Why are we going there? The staff left at 5:00," Tom says in his normal pitch.

The autocab stops abruptly and his body lunges forward in the seat. My palm stretches across his chest to brace for the impact.

"Shall I re-route to another destination?" the autocab says.

"No, please proceed," I say, a little annoyed seeing how always-on listening capability by these automatons sometimes doesn't lead to improved service. "Let's just get there. Then we'll worry about getting in."

On the autocab's dashboard a sensor blink. To the side a screen is scrolling through electronic files. It briefly stops. My picture appears on the left side with my name and Universal ID. It starts again. Stops. Beneath Tom's silhouette the words 'Unidentified Occupant' flashes.

"Is everything alright?"

"Traffic is optimal. Please sit back and enjoy the ride," the car says.

"I'm being scanned," Tom whispers.

"I know. It'll be okay."

We're never getting out this autocab until the Magistrate identifies Tom. At the very least, I'll get a ticket, at the worst, they'll confiscate him as undocumented property. I don't have time for either scenarios.

"Tom, is Xavier still at McKurdles?"

"He is."

"Is Sam on duty?"

"Yes. He's working the midnight shift."

"On my mark, reach into Xavier's electronic wallet on my Pulsometer and replicate his Universal ID unto your system identifier."

"But..."

"Tom, please. Just do as I say."

The autocab slows. Traffic is light. In the rearview a flock of blackbirds head our way.

Sam's number finally comes up on my Pulsometer.

"Hey, Sam."

"Shelly?"

"I'm bummed you're missing our ladies night. Maybe you can break out early or stop by when you get off."

"Hon, you know I wouldn't miss it if it could be helped but you know how easily replaceable some of us are these days. Haven't seen your sexy ass in ages. Your other half's here."

"Is he now?"

"I'll keep an eye on him for ya. Still hunky as ever. You better hold on tight, girl."

"Do me a favor. Take a snapshot of his UI for me. I'm planning a surprise and need a recent photo."

"Give me a minute."

A thought tries to wedge itself in my peacefulness prodding me to say something, confront Xavier about his excessive visits to the bar. Is our happiness a delusion, a front to what truly lies beneath? We're dignified fools afraid of the burden of each other's emotional dumps. Guilt is our shameware. He's either running to or from something.

"Done."

Xavier's UI appears on my Pulsometer. Maybe we're one and the same where denial is my bar.

"You're the best, Sam. Let's catch up soon."

"For sure, baby cakes."

The birds are much larger, closer, flashing red eyes. One breaks out of formation and swoops around the car, stopping at Tom's window. The autocab slows to a crawl.

Tom looks away, then behind the vehicle. "Is everything alright?"

"Now! Tom."

"Done."

The swarm dives low above the autocab's roof. Its sensor quiets and steadies. Beneath Tom's silhouette the words 'Xavier Vinson' appears.

"Hug me."

"Are you alright?"

"Dammit, Tom."

He reaches across the seat and hugs me awkwardly.

The swarm lead snaps a picture and flies off to its next mission. The followers spring into formation and zoom into the sky.

I release him. The autocab resumes normal speed.

"Incoming from Xavier."

"Ignore."

"He wants to speak to you."

"When did you learn to ignore my requests? I can't. Not now."

"He says he knows about the software in your cranial mesh."

Tell me something I don't know—the bad update or the update he made?

"Why don't you open the windows and yell it out for the whole world to hear. Here, let me help you. Window open."

The harsh cold wind blows in. The autocab compensates by increasing the internal temperature.

"You should let Xavier fix this. There's nothing we can do about the EMPs. We should go home."

"You can return on your own if you'd like. See how far you'll get. I have to do this. If there's any care programmed in you, you'll listen and do as I say. I need you."

The sunset is about to give way to night. We both look out our window at the quiet mountainous beauty as we ascend higher and higher into the hills.

"You have two calls from your friends and an incoming from Xavier."

Tom's voice sounds serene in this environment which helps to calm me down. "Tell the girls to have a good time and I'm on my way."

"But, how?" Tom asks.

"Time is linear. As soon as we're done here we'll be on our way," I say.

"And Xavier? He's very close to being plastered."

"Did he leave a message?"

I hope Sam kept his mouth shut. Xavier's voice fills the compartment. Please don't say anything, spicy.

"Hi, babe. I'm on my way back. You better not be asleep when I get there. Remember what I've told you. We can fix this. I love you, babe."

"Did you want to leave a reply?"

Yeah, give you a second chance to play with my head. You had no right messing with my cranial mesh in the first place.

"Tell him we're having a good time and I can't wait for him to get home."

The observatory comes into view high on the mountain.   Signs declare the businesses and establishments up ahead including MemServ.

Vehicles are speeding down the hill in the opposite direction heading to the highway. One other car is up ahead with a bunch of rowdy teens playing loud music.

"What time is it?" I ask.

"four past six. The ETA is 6:08," the autocab says.

MemServ comes into view on the left and it's a massive structure. A bit further down the main road and we arrive at the observatory's visitor entrance.

I open the door and step outside. Tom does the same.

"Wait here for us," I say to the autocab, in case it drives off to find a charging station.

"I think we're being followed. That's the same pair from the airport."

It's no surprise. PHAC is everywhere. There's nothing they can do without some form of warrant. I have nine hours left before the medical warrant is issued or for me to turn myself in.

Tom heads for the visitor entrance. I reach for his hand.

"Who are you visiting?"

He stops and looks at me quizzically.

"The obs..."

"Nope. Follow me."

The signs for the employee entrance are very small in comparison to the ones for the visitor center.

"I have to remind you of the fifth," Tom says.

"I have to remind you you're here to serve and to protect me. Disengage your security module."

"You'll have to provide the executing command."

"WQRD-15966, convert to Rogue Mode."

Tom transforms into the bare metal of an intelligent machine without the human persona. All the control gates are wide open for exploitation though he will only obey my commands and thankfully without any objections or sophisticated reasoning.   His connections back to IxTar are disabled, no backups to remote systems anywhere, no electronic identification, no empathy, just logic.

I wait for his system to reboot to delete any residual memories before we proceed.

An electronic panel is on the door and above it is a camera.

"Scramble all electronic signals in a 50-meter radius."

"Complete."

I'm suddenly warm and a moment overcomes me. It's the déjà vu of being inside the observatory. This time it's familiar for I've seen it in the moment earlier. I remember a wall of spiral staircases with a mechanic's door embedded on the radial wall.

"Expand the scramble for 500-meters."

This should cover the entire building. Again, I'm puzzled how I know this. Is it intuition? We head to the visitor's center passing patrons along the way. The double wood doors are heavy. Everything is toned down to limit reflection and maximize the dark. A cold gust of wind sweeps around me. I pull my jacket up around my neck. The spiral stairs are to the left and they wind around the interior of the massive hollow room. At the top of the staircase is a deck where the powerful telescopes are. We approach the mechanics door. I look around to see if we are being observed but people are in their own world. I turn the handle and it opens. Quickly I slip inside and motion for Rogue Tom to follow before shutting the door.

Boilers are spewing hot steam in the air. Water drips from pipes into concrete gutters. Cobwebs attach to our faces like friendly ghosts as we try to peel them away. Finally, I find it. I pry the grill off the wall and throw it to the side with a clang. The opening is large enough for us to crawl through so I go first, getting on my knees and entering the narrow metallic tunnel.

I'm still getting used to Rogue Tom and his quiet and obedience. A light shine ahead and we head in that direction. Below us is a grill to an office space. I push it down and it swings to one side.

"Follow me," I say to Rogue Tom.

Holding on to the edge I slip backwards through the vent until I'm swinging five feet from the floor. I let go and land on my feet.

I step aside and watch as Rogue Tom does the same. I need basic Tom back to break into the servers and search for the data we need. The only thing is I have no idea what we're looking for.

"WQRD-15666, convert to Stealth Mode."

I wait for the system to reboot and for Tom to come online.

The flutter of his eyelids reminds me of when he first came home not too long ago. He'll have a memory gap that IxTar will think is a malfunction but he's going to have questions. This is the only way an AI-enabled machine can forget, otherwise, they remember everything, even past transgressions that if they were humans, they would hold grudges and judge people without thinking they could change.

"Where, how...?", he says, looking around.

"Never mind. You said this is where the good stuff is. Now help me find it."

"Strange. All electronic signals have been scrambled. They'll restore in ten minutes."

"Then we have eight to find what we came here for."

While he works on the server, I have to plan our exit. Once the signals are restored the alarms blast will alert their security team of the breach. Getting out won't be easy.

I open the door to the room without any problem and walk down the dark hallway. The only doors lead to a mix gender bathroom, a lunch room and the large black door with the lit exit sign above it. I know it leads out to where we started, the employee's entrance.

"Whoa," Tom says.

A doe runs towards me and stops short, close enough for me to pet her. Her fur glistens. Dappled starlight fills the darkened space so it glows like a sunlit day in a meadow. The curdling of the brook below my feet is soothing. I stoop to scoop a handful of the cool liquid to bring to my lips. My skin burns and begins to glow a golden hue. Dappled starlight stream from my pores stopping a few inches from the surface. There's a weightlessness. An unexplained nothingness. I reach for my skin and I'm jolted from the daze.

I walk back into the suite. Tom is busy on the servers, running all five of them at the same time. I let him work and try not to ask questions to interrupt. Two minutes should be enough time to get outside. With three minutes left I want to tell him I had another moment but I think he knows. Is it a true glimpse of the future? Why is this happening?

"Interesting."

I want to know, but he's focused. Two minutes to go.

"Tom."

"The electromagnetic pulse hit the earth's core and propels us forward in time on average three seconds. It goes unnoticed, at least by most. Another anomaly coincides with your moments when the rotation somehow tries to correct itself by jumping back five seconds. That leaves a two second lapse but I'm guessing you're experiencing the entire time shift—the forwards and the reversal. It's like an old grandfather clock that slows down after a while with sporadic jumps and needs to be rewound to keep ticking and moving forward at a constant rate."

"Earth has an internal clock?" I say, understanding he means it figuratively.

"It's conceivable. A human heart beats rhythmically to pump blood through your veins and sustain life. If a heart stops, an electric pulse can restore it, given certain parameters. Computers, machines like me and almost anything mechanical operate on this fundamental concept."

Tom extrapolates his hypothesis while I try to grasp what he's saying in simple terms.

"So, we created computers in our own image with a physical internal clock to keep it alive, so to speak. If earth has an internal clock, it must mean, it was purposely and intelligently created to maintain and sustain life."

"The cyborg chip in your cranial mesh is affected by the time lapse and is trying to account for the gaps by filling in events from your past and predicting the likeliest future scenarios so it'll have a complete memory to upload."

"How would it derive scenes that fit so perfect that's not jarring and nonsensical that they flow seamlessly into reality? We're missing something."

"The human mind is a puzzle no one will ever solve. I wonder what's the source of these random spurts and why it's affecting you and not cyborgs or other automata?"

"What about the who? Who is doing this?" I say.

"It could all be random. If you consider earth is being pummeled by all kinds of radiation, meteors, particles, interstellar objects on a regular basis. It really is a miracle it has warded off dangerous impacts. It's almost like it's protected."

"Like it was meant to be," I say, as he turns to the servers again. I grab his arm. "We have to go."

I check my Pulsometer and we're over by a minute. With only 1 minute to exit the building I hope we get out before the system comes back online and the alarm sounds.

"Why the rush? How did you get the doors open?"

Tom stops in his tracks to relieve his new suspicions. If it was his namesake, he would have already run out the building.

"We have to go, Tom. If anything, I take full responsibility, okay?"

"What do you mean?"

I pause to look in the direction where I'd seen the secured steel door. The narrow concrete walkway is there instead with manicured landscape on both sides. The promise of home, fresh air and our freedom calls to me. It's all clear, we're good to go.

"Let's go!"

I run down the barely lit hall with all my might savoring the victory of beating the clock. A quick glance behind me and Tom is in tow.

My body crashes into something cold and solid.

"Shelly."

I get to my feet and push my weight with all my might to dislodge the horizontal bar. The heavy door slams against the concrete wall and sticks. Dark, angry shadows come out of nowhere.

A hot fiery blast pierces my chest.

"Shelly!"

My body bathes in a quickly expanding warm river that radiates from my middle in search of a tributary.

Flowing in multiple directions the weighty liquid floods and pull me under into a thick frigid darkness. There's no fight. My will is no longer my own. I speed through the watery bliss. Tom's handsome face fades with the light.

PART 1 - SPACE

❧✦☙

15 DARGAV

"There you are.   Welcome home, Cassiopeia."

I'm contained, restrained and agitated.

"You're surely an excitable one. We're almost through the worse of it. Some say it's like the first time exiting a mother's womb, but without the screams."

Slowly the person who spoke comes into view. A pixelated holographic ethereal object floats in the shape of a woman's body. I look at her from head to toe. Another pair of pixelated feet is below me. Pixelated legs, abdomen. I reach for my face and my pixelated arm goes through it.

Spinning, I'm slammed into a pliable membrane that traps, energizes and catapults me to the opposite side where I ricochet like a boomerang. Over and over again the container that protects and holds me together catalyzes my movement so faster and faster I go in no discernable pattern. I don't know how to slow down, how to stop.

"Calm down. You need to focus." she says, standing further from me like I'm a danger. "It's all about balance and control".

Her voice is soothing, confident and a bit distracted but filled with empathy. It's working. The room comes into view. I look around the large, dimly lit enclosure. Other pixelated bodies are restrained in tall black metallic containers while pixelated nurses attend to them. "Good. It's a natural reaction. You're getting it. Just try to relax."

"What's going on? Where am I? Where's Tom?"

"Everything will be alright. It's a little adjustment for first timers."

I struggle to free myself from the restraints.

"After the briefing things will become clearer."

The restraints exhale and I'm free to move my bodily container.

"You can call me Mirna. Follow me. This won't take long."

She watches me as I take a step and then another. A sense of weightlessness and serenity overpowers me.

"Where are we going?"

Wherever this is, it's massive, clinical and orderly. Another pixelated person is in the area where Mirna stops. Vast glass windows are on one side and I'm reminded of the Genesis. The environment is poorly lit and gives off a frigid cold feel. Pixelated bodies glisten in a variety of colors and shimmer. Iridescent colors I have no name for bounce around inside bodily containers. I imagine I look the same.

Mirna points to a flat round object on an electrical platform. "Place your hand here. It won't cause discomfort."

My pixelated hand senses another force pushing it back so it doesn't slip through the panel.

"You're doing great. Won't take but a moment."

My mind latches on the word 'moment' and I remember: Tom and I run to the exit of the Pollinova Observatory. Upon opening the door two armed guards with weapons drawn greet us. Without any warning they shoot. A bullet exits their weapon exploding in my chest. I fall to the floor. Tom calls for me but I can't answer. I want to tell him to run but I'm sinking, being pulled into a warm, lovely embrace. His face fades. A baby cries out. The doctor in blue garb administers it. 'It's a girl', she says, and wrap a blanket around the newborn then hands it to the disheveled woman on a hospital bed. While nurses take care of her, she smiles at the child, holds it close to her bosom. Her face comes into view. Mom. The scene changes like a movie. A little girl is riding a tricycle. She giggles as she rides away from a man who had given the back seat a little shove. She glances back at him and he smiles joyfully. 'Not so fast, Shelly.' I don't remember dad being that young. I giggle, look at me go, Dad. Faster and faster, further away, smaller and smaller he gets. I'm afraid. I can't stop. The pedal overpowers my legs and the tricycle overturns. 'Shelly!'. My father's arms are extended as he smiles proudly and walk towards me graduating from high school, and then college. I hadn't thought of Ian in a long while and there he is feeding me a spoon of ice cream from a mug we share. Xavier's face is a sight for sore eyes on our date in Santa Fe. A phantom pulse pounds in my left chest. My friends Felicia, Georgina, Sam and Viola are at a local club having girl fun. Darkness. Flashing lights. Kirk appears out of a sudden mist and reaches for me. He disappears. My phantom chest pulsates. Scenes from the Genesis and the IxTar boardroom streams by and finally, Tom. His lips mouthing my name. I don't know what this is.

Mirna stands in front of me. "Yes and no." She smiles and there's years of experience in her eyes. "Don't mind me. It's usually the first question a bry asks after a lengthy pause. Hmm. This is a first. Our commander wants to see you, immediately."

A cold feeling overpowers me with memories of Kirk and the Genesis. *Could Tom be doing this, playing with my mind? Has the cranial mesh erupted?*

We walk outside the room and questions I had yet to ask were being supplied with answers electronically. It's as if a frequently asked questions list was uploaded in my mind and the answers available at my whim. Getting one answer led to many more branches of questions.

"Each bry must be triaged before being seen here at the Waystation. It's our welcoming bay for those returning to us and the ones who are new, like you. It's one stop away from home. A first time coming home. Once you've been processed you are free to resume your life."

I'm trying to keep up with her as she traverses the ship and the barrage of new information flooding my mind. "What do mean?"

"Welcome," a man says as a group of pixelated bodies pass us. I turn to look at them, shimmery, iridescent, normalized, calm.

"Once you've served your time on E0, you return here to prepare for the trip home. This goes for all prisoners and Neophytes."

"E0."

"E0 was created with everything to sustain life and serve as a penal colony for our most dangerous criminals. Prisoners are sent to E0 or planet earth as some like to call it, to live out a full life sentence. When they've served their time, they return here. Whether they proceed home or are denied re-entry and sent back to the prison is all determined here on the Waystation after their evaluation. "

"You think earth is a prison?"

"Stuck in a body made of disgusting organic materials. Lipids, minerals and tissue that easily succumb to diseases and require major upkeep, necessitating nourishment in short supply or poisonous. Residing in tiny physical structures inches away from the next being; breathing in expelled and toxic matter that slowly gnaws at them so their physical structure disintegrates to natural elements? Prisoners work more than 80% of their time, are allowed to use only 10% of their brains and are prohibited from leaving their solar system. That doesn't sound like freedom to me. It's the perfect penal system for wayward Dargavians."

That word is popping up all over my mind.

"Dargav?"

"Home. We'll leave this solar system when all of earth's humans and prisoners have transitioned, then tunnel our way to Dargav's galaxy."

I want to giggle at the absurdity but things are happening to me internally I sense have a hint of possibility. At least this dream is better than being chased by a crazy misguided machine.

"Transitioned?"

"Birth and re-birth. During both transformations accrued thoughts are removed. Because they're without thoughts or thoughtless they're called brys. Brys are processed here on the Waystation in preparation for Dargav. "

"What does Dargav look like?"

She stops at a dense pixelated structure solidified by an opposing force.

"Like the eyes you had on earth."

She places her hand on a panel. It slides open to reveal a vestibule with another double door on the opposite side made of amorphous matter. "The commander is inside. When he's done, you're free to roam the ship. Oh, one more thing. Remember I said on earth prisoners use no more than 10% of their brains? On Dargav, we use all of it. In a few hours you'll experience fluid thought with a clarity like nothing you've ever experienced. It'll be like you absorbed a library or databank. You'll be able to answer your own questions and experience a boundless existence. Don't keep him waiting."

I motion to the dense pixelated structure and it clears to reveal a large enclosure, like a spacious office suite. Pixelated equipment and computers are in the middle of the room. This is like nothing I've ever seen, not even in a flash.

"Cassiopeia, welcome to Dargav. I'm commander Rahab, of the ISV Exodus."

An amorphous pixelated humanoid walk towards me and bows slightly. There'd be no use trying to shake hands. I bow slightly in return.

"Nice to meet you."

"Yes, yes. Your signature is truly Vyotrian. Your ancestors will be notified you'll be joining them. I trust Mirna has given you the Neophyte briefing."

"She has."

"Good, good. How exciting it must be for you to finally know what it means to exist."

"It's a lot to take in," I say, sensing the continued bombardment of new information in my mind I don't know what to do with. So, now I know Dargav is 6 trillion AUs from the penal colony. Dargavian prisoners lose their ability to shift states and can only be pure solid matter, weighted down by carbon and other common elements. They become humanized where their Dargavian memories become inaccessible allowing them to blend in on earth. Like other humans they can use at most 10% of their processing capacity, their brain. They live a life of their choosing depending on luck or hard work without any of the benefits or knowledge of their Dargavian roots. Earth death is the transitional state that signifies a release from earth life at the conclusion of their served time. The length of time varies depending on the crime. Suicide is a revolving door to another life sentence on earth. Punishment includes limited thinking which itself is a container, so is a human body, so is living on the planet, so is living within this tiny solar system. E0 is an unsupervised penal colony, except for being controlled by time. It's a highly sophisticated and well-protected ecosystem guarded from internal and external forces and threats. Humans are allowed to explore but never beyond their solar system. Dargavian prisoners blend in with humans and have children that are called Neophytes when they go home for the first time.

"You're being enlightened," he says.

"Pardon?"

"The new information you're privy to. You've transitioned from having a human brain to a Vellum processor. The capability is only limited by your lack of creativity. You'll have access to answers for most of your questions. Some you'll have to derive for yourself using the information available. Once verified you'll add that knowledge to our data bank. That's how we teach and share with each other."

The pause seems awkward but we both have a lot to process. He steps closer.

"Would you consider going back?"

Is that a trick question? Do atomics play mind games too, like humans?

"Is that an option?"

"Yes and no."

I'm trying to grasp this, wake up from this, get my head to stop being inundated with information. Things I don't even think is relevant hit my processor like a sandstorm. Why would I need to know how to restore a Millivac Capacitor? What's a Millivac Capacitor?

He walks to one of the vast windows as meteors stream by.

"I understand a lot is coming at you all at once. I promise it will make sense in a short while," he says. "Cassiopeia, we are in dire need of an enlightened Vyotrian to help us with a crisis."

"I don't understand."

"E0 as we know it is headed for a catastrophe. Our best chance to avert it is for someone from your ancestral line to reset the primordial axis that controls earth time."

The ship slowly decelerates.   Outside, bright shining stars and interstellar objects litter the dark space. I'm reminded of the Baltimore Aquarium as fish and sea creatures of varying size and shape float in a multitude of directions, their bodies reflect a source of light against a black background.

Inching to stand beside him I get a better look while querying my built-in library for more on primordial axis and how it affects earth. Vyotrians are the only Dargavians entrusted with earth's time. There are no instructions how it's done.

"It would only be temporary and you'd need to return within 24-hours."

"Why the rush?"

"It's the nature of the transition. There are four phases every bry and Neo goes through: Neonatal,

Deniability, Febrile and Normalization. You're in the first stage. The second stage will begin within two hours of the first. Your core will rupture if it's not stabilized during the Febrile stage. It begins 24-hours after re-born. Normalization erases all thoughts and memories so you're able to become your full self without the emotional burdens of earth life. Of the four phases, the Febrile is the most delicate."

"I thought this was life eternal."

"We're made of atoms with a nucleonic core. The most powerful and natural energy source there is but it must be stabilized during the Febrile phase. If you're in earth's atmosphere during this time you'll disintegrate. If you're beyond the ionosphere, you'll supernova prematurely. Normalization is when you've adapted and acclimated within the Dargav environment. I want you to promise you'll do everything you can to return to us within 12-hours of reaching earth, even if the mission fails. It's in your atoms, Cassiopeia. You come from a long line of Dargavians. The finest and most loyal. You'd do us an insurmountable favor."

I'm not doing this. I always wake up from my dreams.

His silence gnaws at me like an unspoken conversation.

What if by some crazy chance this time I don't wake up, what would the Dargavians think of me for all eternity if I didn't help them when I could? That would be a prison. And forever. He said it was only for a little while, then I could return. And, if all this is not a dream—I left something precious behind. I didn't say goodbye.

"I think you need to fill me in."

"Forty years ago, Dargav had a falling out with some of its citizens when a high ranking official, Smiloff, was convicted of his crimes and sent to E0 to serve a life sentence. Bandits who objected joined together and started a civil war. We managed to capture them and was about to send them to E0 to serve their time as humans when they stole a ship and escaped. For years these Bandits hop about from one galaxy to another looking for E0. Because we managed to lockdown half their processing capability, their abilities and technologies are not as sophisticated as ours but they're improving. Lately, we detected an unusual amount of electromagnetic radiation directed at E0's crust. Every burst disrupts the normal earthly rhythms that maintains ecological and physiological symbiosis. It speeds up the earth's rotation, distorts its axis, and thwarts the synchronization of time. We've managed to revert the effects so far but if the disruption exceeds 10 seconds it will lead to a gradual and widespread awakening or enlightening of the Dargavian prisoners. Our galactic neighbors know the importance of protecting earth at all costs. This leaves the Bandits who are undoubtedly responsible for these bursts."

"How can you be sure?"

"If they awaken Smiloff he'll unlock the other half of their brains and they'll remember where and how to find Dargav. With Smiloff as their leader, Dargav will have an onslaught of its enlightened criminals wage war. Since we can't locate the Bandits, our only defense is to fix the jump in time and restore the symbiosis. We've been sending Hurtchins, our primary horologists to adjust the time sync but his ship was captured by the military arm of the humans and he's trapped in the ship held in one of their secure facilities. Every minute spent on earth he loses processing power and his strength drops incrementally. It's a built-in failsafe for atomics so we're not tempted to dominate the humans. Our bodies will slowly morph, becoming carbon-based; processing power will eventually dwindle to match a human's intellect if our visits are prolonged on the planet."

"Like Cinderella."

"Who? Oh."

He turns his back to the window and draws up a hologram of a derry, a small ship large enough for a dozen crew members, used to make short intergalactic runs. Equipped with a nuclear fusion core it synthesizes hydrogen for power and stacked with limited weaponry it achieves a max warp speed of 15 mach.

A scanning white light across the ship's body stops on the aft flange.

"Normally, our ships are undetectable in earth's solar system, but Hurtchins' was sabotaged."

"Any idea who?"

"Someone on Dargav purposely caused the modulator located here to combust upon entering earth's ionosphere disabling the cloak mechanism."

The paused white light blinks incrementally faster. It turns red, triggering an alarm. Commander Rahab disengages it.

"Hurtchins and the ship are being held in one of Space Force's facilities. He may be hurt, but we can't risk the secrets of time being divulged even to another Dargavian. That's why we need a Vyotrian to go to his location and break him out."

He looks at me. This would be a good time to wake up but with no Kirk or cyborg chasing me, falling into a bottomless black pit or Xavier to shake me, I'm stuck.

"I want to help, but, this isn't my forte."

"It'll be as simple as Pollinova."

"What do you mean?"

"We review our Neos and bry's life history to see how they've fared on earth, to see if they're suitable for rehabilitation or have any hidden talents."

"Pollinova was a mistake. It got me...here."

"A mistake? Every action taken or bypassed is a way forward, to what's next, but I won't judge. Curiosity is a potent thing. Where would humans be without it? You'll return in your current state. The advantage is you'll be undetectable. All you have to do is get within ten feet of Hurtchins and he'll become re-enlightened and able to complete his mission. You return together when he's through."

I must be stuck in one of those simulations from the Genesis. Accepting this mission has got to be my way back to reality, the way I wake up. A remnant of a memory comes through loud and clear: *Face it.*

"The Deniability phase will kick in and you'll start doubting whether any of this is real even though you have access to all the proof in your processor. Your earth brain will question whether you're in a dream or losing your mind. I assure you, this is real. Accept the mission. That's the best way for you to prove to yourself there is more than life on earth."

Shake me, Xavier.

"This Hurtchins, if freed will fix the clock and prevent the awakening of humans?"

"Yes. You'll go back with a team who will take you to where Hurtchins is being held. They'll repair the ionosphere shields so bursts won't get through damaging the earth and cause harm to the humans."

"How long until the Bandits know whether they've found the real E0?"

"They're disrupting the planet as we speak. If they fire another burst and the core jumps another five seconds before it's fixed, the awakening will begin. Smiloff could emerge within hours with the know-how to get their misguided band back together."

16 EO

Any minute now I'll wake up and I'll be wrapped in Xavier's arms and Tom will be off in the next room doing his thing. But all around me is a flurry of activities to get the Tellurium ready for a mission to earth. It's a crew of six. I make seven. My processor is growing with more information. I take tiny sips. The crew are skilled in repairing earth's shields. All that knowledge is available to me but my role for now is to be a passenger.

The coordinates they're holding Hurtchins is near Nevada. Everything is all set. No need to worry about security cameras, access codes, breaking in through HVAC systems or mechanical closets. I'm simply instructed to walk in and get within ten feet of Hurtchins. He'll be freed, he'll fix the clock then we return together in his freed impounded ship. The prisoners lack the technology to see under the hood but it will work for us.

It's been several earth hours now since I've transitioned and about a month since I was shot. Xavier and Tom must be out of their minds with grief. It's bitter sweet to leave them and see this new world. New galaxy. The Deniability stage comes with an emotional dampener where phantom grief tries to make me sad, cry, but I can't give in to my human brain. Why grieve if it's not real and I'll wake up soon?

I follow the commander to the out-processing section that's on the other side of the ship. It has two bays. One for prisoners being sent to earth in a compressed state to serve their prison sentence. All memory of Dargav has been secured in a dormant state away from the active portion of their processor which is reduced to 10% capacity. They've been given a blank slate to live a normal human life. They'll replenish the dwindling humans and possibly save the human race from extinction.

The other bay is for amorphous atomics—the words they use to describe our pixelated state—who can travel anywhere in the universe unobstructed, shifting as we deem. On earth, they have no way yet of detecting atomics as most of the natural elements we're made of aren't on earth or mentioned in their periodic table. Our presence goes undetectable, unnoticed. Hurtchins' ship being sabotaged allowed earth's most sophisticated and highest radar technology to pick up his ship on a very low frequency. Even though some humans claimed they've seen something it will be denied and soon forgotten. Forgetting is so human, they need it to survive for remembering everything would drive them crazy. It's what the atomics count on that with 10% brain utilization it'll help Dargavian prisoners coexist with humans, stay busy trying to solve the trivial until their time's up.   With the awakening they'll easily put the pieces together and know there's more to the limited life they've been forced to live.

Don't return to San Francisco. The last order from the commander reverberates in my mind. This mission is too important and I'd never do anything to jeopardize it. I won't be able to tell the love of my life goodbye.

Holy shit. I can choose to be male or female or neither; a particle or wave or a combination.

One of the crew members motions for me to follow. Out of habit I'm thinking about travel clothes, luggage, passport and reservations, but I no longer have a need for those material things.

We enter a ginormous hanger.   Derries dock in each of the ten launch pads. They have a solid round center and five metallic branches spaced evenly like fisted arms extending ten feet from the center.   I expected to see flashing lights or even strobe but no major fanfare. We're on the floor of the hangar and the team up ahead ascends to the center via a light beam reminiscent of a reverse waterfall.   One by one they disappear into the belly of the ship until it's my turn.

I walk beneath the portal and immediately whatever sense of a body I had left over from my years on earth is shattered. Merging with the light beam I'm flooded with a sense of warmth and expansion like swimming in powerful rapids. My atoms shoot upwards as it ascends towards the ship. My form is reshaped and I'm gently lowered to the ship's floor. Without the need to sit, I take the empty chamber beside Lenali, the crew member who has been the friendliest.

The entry closes and a series of sounds like locks on doors go on until a whirring drown out all the other sounds. On a screen of the outside, fisted arms spin slowly, then quickly accelerate at a high revolution. It makes the ship appear solid and circular. All around the interior are holographic screens depicting various solar systems, ship status and readouts of the twelve protective layers that surround earth. They're all showing damage from the bursts that have punched a hole or fractured more than half of them since the last repair.

"We'll get you to your location in 5 million AUs or five earth hours. It will take us another earth hour to repair the throttle and the tympanic modulator. When they find out who sabotaged that ship, they'll be sent for eternal death."

"I thought there was no death," I said, feeling like someone just ran a bait and switch on me.

"When earth is too good for some prisoners there is an eternal death. Their processors are wiped and they become brys," Lenali says.

"Like a megalith or zombie," I say out loud before I could stop myself. And here I am heading to earth to stop the opposite of a zombie apocalypse—mass enlightenment.

"Worse than a zombie. A zombie still has reflexes. It's been 2,000 earth years since the last awakening. It started in Rome, then Greece and spread worldwide. The humans then built massive complex structures with their new knowledge that modern man is still trying to unravel. The Vyotrian has always been the only ones to keep watch, so to speak," Lenali says. "Enough history lessons. You should enter low power mode. We'll give you a shake when we're close."

It never occurred to me sleep would be different but of course it is. And for power, atoms only depend on each other to keep them energized, in optimal state. A degradation begins with no atomic interaction.

I don't want to miss a thing so I watch as they navigate the ship, make course corrections and plan the repair job. It's a new technology to harden the shields and make them even more impervious to radiation.

"If we add a deflector here it will absorb the radiation and when it gets to 100 PHz it will reverse course and detonate the source like a heat seeking missile," Burniv says, pointing to the ringed simulation of a shield covering earth about a hundred miles or so into the ionosphere. "And it will tell us exactly the location of the source."

"Let's do it. If it works it will slow them down if they're not captured first," Lenali says. He looks at me with a parental smirk, though I sense he transitioned at a younger age than I, and engage my low power mode. "Re-enlightening Hurtchins will drain your energy. If you want to make it back, you must be at full power."

It's a dream state. I can still see what they're doing but the urge to analyze what they're saying, look it up in my databanks or try to come up with a solution to the problems has lost the urge of curiosity. I look inward and my processor is at 100%. I'm able to absorb, retain and understand more, come up with better solutions and implement them according to a logical plan. So far, I've come across five solutions that can help the humans on earth from global poverty to disease management to the ongoing water crisis. But, I'm forbidden from interfering in human problems. Dargavians and the atomicized believe these puzzles bring meaning to human and prisoner lives and make their time go by faster. All problems serve a purpose.

My power is suddenly back to full force. Lenali and the crew are watching as the ship approach the most beautiful blue and green marble I've come to know as earth, now E0. I wonder if they still marvel at their creation.

A searing heat ray zings past the ship and slams into the planet. The ship spins violently, vibrates, loses power and is immersed in total darkness as it hurtles forward.

"Nuclear generators will be online in a second. That was close," Lenali says.

"That can't be good. A second hit before repairs are made will throw it over the threshold," Burniv says.

The power comes back on and the screens and holograms resume their display. The ship is once again on course.

Lenali swipes on one virtual screen and then another. "I'm getting a reading. Time sync is eight seconds."

Burniv generates holograms and select portions of the screen to enlarge or drilldown for more information. "The damage is way more than we planned. We'll have to call for reinforcement."

"Full throttle to the drop point."

"Tellurium, we're getting reports a strike barely missed you."

The voice is familiar as it fills the ship's interior.

"We're back on full power, Commander, but the damage to the shields are more severe than we anticipated. Could be another hour or two of work," Lenali says.

"Glad to hear you're all okay. Glad to hear. Reinforcements are on the way. Let me know when Cassiopeia has been delivered. Signing off."

The ship bursts through earth's atmosphere and zips across the Pacific, over a mountainous area resembling the Grand Canyon and then a deserted stretch of land. It slows as it approaches a ginormous building resembling an airport without the runways with nothing around it except for one road and two guard towers and a giant sign that reads "Red Rock Private Property, Keep Out" on the roof.

"Cassiopeia, this is where the Tellurium leaves you. Hurtchins and his ship are in the facility. I trust you know what to do?"

I nod, hoping if this is a dream at least when I awake, I'll be alive and earth will be its usual wonderful messed up state with the only thing to worry about is AI gaining sentience.

The belly opens. I approach the edge of the platform. A light beam absorbs my atoms then rearranges them before placing me on the ground. The warmth and sinking feeling as I'm ricocheting through light reminds me of how this all got started— exiting Pollinova.

The belly closes and the ship zip off, disappearing into the sky.

Looking down at my pixelated feet as I head towards the structure, I'm pleased there are no footprints.

"Hi there," I say to the guard at the gate. His ominous weaponry is almost the length of his body. He looks up briefly then returns to scouring a motion screen with a miniaturized view of ice hockey playing in one corner.

Five hundred feet further is the entrance to the building.

A bright light flare streaks across the sky and disappears. My processor identifies it as a mega radiation burst from outer space. The guard at the gate doesn't move. It's undetectable to humans and their devices will think it's a shooting star or small meteor. If it's another burst from the Bandits, the threshold has been breached.

I enter the cavernous rooms moving as quickly as I can through the single level facility, but no ship. My power drops by three percent. Did they make a mistake? I run up a mezzanine level hoping to get a bird's eye view of the facility but there's nothing here except for space junk and a few people milling about.

Behind me is a huge window array. The sun is glaringly hot though I'm not bothered by it. A swirly heat wave outside catches my attention. There it is again, a spatial disturbance resembling heat radiating off the desert floor. I follow the wave and it makes a giant arc then dissipates. Another wave emerges and follows the same path.

I exit the mezzanine and return outside to where I saw the wave. It's quiet except for the howling wind shifting sand and dust piles around as it beats against an invisible object. I approach it and poke my pixelated finger where sand piles up. Mirrored dense particles strung together by low frequency waves distorts the air. I look it up in my processor. It's probably used to dampen sound and radar detection. I take a step forward. My body passes through the electron curtain. Inside the hangar, the ship sits on tall shiny steel beams jutting though the ground stopping upwards fifteen feet. No one is here. On this side, the interior is a solid black. The derry is a replica of the one I travelled on. It's covered in sand and dust and surrounded by heavy drilling machines. I get under the belly.

"Hello?"

It remains shut.

The steel beams have small evenly spaced ridges on them that stops half-way up. My hand goes through the pole. I look up how to solidify myself so I don't permeate the steel. The silica mixed with hydrogen can form a thin shell to cover me. I derive an isotope to fuse to my external membrane.   My hand bounces off the surface. Reaching for the highest ridge I pull myself up onto the beam and climb as high as there are ridges to hold my feet. The shell begins to crack and fall away.

"Hurtchins?"

My power rapidly drops to 65%. Then 55%.

There's a sound, but the shell dissipates and I float to the ground.

A shuffle fills the quiet followed by a loud exhalation. The belly slides open. I step into the beam.

17 THE CLOCK FIXER

A pixelated man approaches. It's difficult to tell age but I sense he's older. He looks me over, scans me.

"A Vyotrian. And a Neophyte, and already in the field. Folks call me Hurtchins. Sorry for taking so much of your power but I was down to 20. We don't have much time. The threshold has been breached."

"What happens now?" I say, following him as he walks over to a holographic kiosk and types.

"We fix it and pray to the stars the awakening can be contained; otherwise, there'll be no peace."

The whirring of the fisted arms disrupts the cloaking waves used to disguise the location of the ship. Above us the clear blue sky appears.

He enters information into the systems and appears deep in thought. "Ready?" he says finally, then heads to the front port.

The ship takes off flying across the desert, low, then high. A populated area with palm trees appears in the distance. The ground below is blurred then there's nothing but white light and a steady zing.

"I take it you're not just here to juice me up. We have three stops to make in a very short period of time so you might want to pay close attention. The first is the center wheel."

The information is already blasting across my processor the second I come across a term I haven't heard before.

"It's a term we use to help Neos understand the mechanism behind earth's symbiosis. If you think of a clock, it has a big hand, a small hand, and a pendulum. The center wheel is the underlying mechanism that moves the big hand to signify hours. The six major oceans are our center wheel, the big hand. The third wheel relies on energy from the center wheel to signify minutes. It's the small hand. Every ten seconds an ocean sends energy particles to the next closest ocean to the right alternating positive and negative energy to generate a current. Starting with the South Pacific Ocean since it's warmer and atoms are already in a kinetic state, these atoms are attracted to this here Millivac Capacitator. As we grab onto the oceanic current and it mixes with the Millivac, a flywheel effect resets the oceanic current as we continue north then end at the Southern Ocean. Six rotations are one earth minute and sixty is one earth hour."

"It's like Alice in Wonderland."

"Where do you think all these stories come from? Humans may only use 10% of their processor but they make very good use of it. All the major bodies of water on earth are connected for a reason. Humans vastly underestimate the power of the ocean's current but if its disrupted, the primordial axis shifts and life is disrupted. Right now, the current runs slower than it should and needs synchronization. We're approaching the South Pacific."

The apparatus he calls the Millivac Capacitor buzzes and spins displaying a multitude of light infused colors. Hurtchins is focused so I walk around the ship's interior stopping at a kiosk. A light suddenly blinks a steady red. My processor displays a sequence of characters to correct the situation.

"Hurtchins."

He ignores me. I look at the kiosk, the red light blinks faster. Before I could stop myself, I enter the sequence. The light returns to a steady green.

Quietly we zip across the large ocean. On the screen the North Pacific Ocean comes into view, then the North Atlantic, South Atlantic, Indian and Southern.

The apparatus stops spinning and settles on a bright green color.

"Now we head to the escape wheel, the pendulum. If the current travels too fast to maintain equilibrium, the escape wheel tries to slow it down. Unfortunately, there's no way to speed it up so time jumps ahead without intervention. That's why we need to reset and why we're coming to a stop over the Pinnacles Desert."

Below us and all around for miles are numerous piles of golden sand and stone pillars that look like a stone city for stone people. I shudder recalling the commanders warning if I don't return in time. They vary in height and size, conical, with the tallest extending about 20 feet in the air. A gust of wind blows mounds of sand against the pillars bathing them in the glistening beam of the sun.

"With the help of the wind and gravity, this is earth's pendulum."

"What do we do here?"

"Nothing, thankfully. As long as the humans haven't built any structures to interfere with the wind passing through these pillars, resetting the oceanic current is all we need to do. So, if you haven't figured it out yet, let me introduce myself. In earth terms, I'm your paternal great grandfather's grandfather. Horology is our specialty and maybe you'll be the next to take the reins."

"This is impossible."

"Everything is impossible, until you find a way. What's your name?"

"Shelly. They call me Cassiopeia for some reason."

"Not for any old reason." He walks away to check on a reading. "Whenever I come here, I like to take a moment, to pay homage to the ancestors."

"So, are we done? Crisis averted?" I ask.

He ignores me and walks over to one of the holograms, looks at it closely, then glance at the apparatus set on a steady green. He rushes to another monitor blinking a symbol. An alarm sounds. He rushes to another monitor, then a kiosk and quickly type information. Another alarm from another system blares. The ship is suddenly embalmed in total black. The whirring of the fisted arms gradually slows until they're frozen in place and eerily quiet except for the howling wind outside. My power drops to 40%.

"This can't be. This can't be."

18 THE BANDIT AND THE BEANSTALK

We are frozen in mid-air. Hurtchins keeps repeating the same 'it can't be' phrase. I'm not sure what's happening, what happened or what exactly 'can't be'. I decide to wait until he addresses me and for now stay out of his way, out of his mind.

"Autosarcophagy."

He murmurs while pacing the length of the ship. I can still see him in the pitch dark. A benefit of our atoms. I wonder if I should mention my power is down to 35%. Anything below 20 and I'll be in a vegetative state like Hurtchins was when I found him. Maybe he could give me a boost.

"Did you see it? The flash of light right before we lost power?"

He stops near me. I'm afraid to look at him not sure what his aura will tell me.

"No. No, I didn't."

"Only a Dargavian laser could disable the atomic fusion. Why would they fire on their own ship?"

"What's going on, Hurtchins?"

I got the nerve to ask at the risk of sounding new.

"Pick any number of words that means the same as betrayal, ungrateful, treachery, mutiny, perfidy. After all we've done."

"The Dargavians have attacked us?"

"And left us to rot in this tin can."

"Now might not be a good time to say this but my power is down to 30%."

"That's impossible. We both should have achieved maximum power once the ship came online," he says, freezing his pace. "Of the most disgusting, human, disagreeable thing!"

He sinks to the floor in a pile of atoms. I'm still getting used to my new body and new capabilities so I crawl my databank for instructions on reading another Dargavian. Got something. I get closer to Hurtchins and scan his atoms. 25% percent.

"What now? We both are heading below the uplink threshold."

"The only thing we can do—wait."

I take that to mean we need a helping hand from another Dargavian, the way I was sent to earth to help him. I didn't know how to tell him for a brief moment, right before the ship froze, I entered a sequence of characters on one of the control panels.

A slight vibration rocks the ship.

"You feel that?" I ask.

He's non-responsive. I feel it again, this time stronger. A sound like a sardine can opening fills the hull then a tiny speck of light shines from the belly.

"Hurtchins, I think they're here.   We're being rescued."

The belly opens wide and without ship power the tractor beam is activated. I inch closer to Hurtchins, not sure why.

They arrive on board one by one.   Three Dargavians. I move towards them to welcome them on board.

"Hi, I'm Shelly. I mean Cassio.."

"Cassiopeia, they don't care or need to know who you are."

Hurtchins voice is stern, weak, as he scrambles to stand. I step back sensing a chill in the air.

"After all these years, finally," one of them says. "You hid this planet well."

"Dhaka," Hurtchins say with scorn. "Crawl back under the rock you've been hiding, you traitorous bastard!"

"Now, now.   Is that any way to speak to your brother? We come in peace. Don't we, brothers? Then again, we came for you and the ship, but... your unexpected companion, on the other hand, is the miracle we've been waiting for."

He walks over to me, inspecting from top to bottom as he circles my form.

"I think she's a Neo," Dhaka says to the one closest to Hurtchins.

"I've never seen one.   Scan her memories for anything we can use."

"Stay away from her!" Hurtchins calls, like a ferocious protector. "No matter what you do to us they'll never let you near Dargav, ever."

What could they do to us?   Immortality has its benefits, right? Wasn't Hurtchins exaggerating when he mentioned rotting?

"What's this new lifeform on earth?" the one scanning me says. "It walks, talks, reasons, but not human?"

"Let me see," Dhaka, who appears to be the leader says. "Incredible. They're developing faster than anticipated to create such marvel. I must see up close. We're taking her with us. By the time they find you, we'll be long gone."

"You don't have to do this. The commander will negotiate your terms.   Release the lock on the atomic fusion and I'll bring him online," Hurtchins says.

"You're barking up the wrong tree. Only the atomic who initiated it can unlock it," Dhaka says.

"Then order them to release it," Hurtchins barks.

"It wasn't one of us."

"We used a Vyotrian beacon to do the work for us. Looks like someone forgot to lock their hatch."

Hurtchins eyes tear into me.

"Cassiopeia,   did   you   complete   your indoctrination?"

"What indoctrination?"

"The phases. Did you complete all your phases before coming here?"

"I entered Deniability about six earth hours ago."

"And they sent you here without securing your interfaces? You hacked a Neo, how could you?"

"A Vyotrian is a Vyotrian. It was meant for you, clock master. No wonder the beacon failed on our other attempts. You've found a way to deny it access to your system. Impressive. No matter, we got what we needed to help us get to the next step of our plan. After waiting so many years, the awakening has begun. Nothing can stop us now."

"So, it's true. That's what this is all about. Throwing time off to sabotage the synchronization to free our prisoners. Do you realize it'll have no effect on you? Your processor lock can only be removed on Dargav. You'll remain at 50% processing power while these humans and cyborgs quickly surpass you. You think they'll let you rule over them with lesser intelligence?" Hurtchins says.

"If this species is what I think it is, I have no need for humans, or desire to rule them or would want to remain on this planet. And why would I ever need to negotiate with Rahab when I can make him kneel? Rot peacefully."

"Cassiopeia, they've betrayed our galaxy, your home. Don't help them."

He lunges for me. Pixels going through pixels before he crashes to the floor. I rush to his side. My processor picks up a new module. I scan him. He's at 20%. Where did his energy go?

The infamous Bandits got the awakening started. I need to know their next move.

We beam down to the sand and then up to their ship. It's a later generation derry. The ISV-Lutetium. They choose to continue with it rather than take Hurtchins', the ISV-Polari, the latest in the Dargav fleet.

A Dargavian, older, in charge, is on board. He observes me.

"What's this? I sent you for the Vyotrian!"

He stands and approaches us as the last one beams onboard.

Dhaka steps forward.

"You wanted a Vyotrian, Kitral! You've got a Vyotrian, plus it's a Neophyte with an unlocked Moduli and has memories of earth you should see."

He steps closer. I can feel Kitral in my processor. The ship is quiet except for the machinery.

"A new lifeform. Evolution is overrated. What's the use of this to us? How will this get us back to Dargav? The older one is worth more as a ransom."

"Kitral, don't you see? All this time the unlocked Moduli we detected was her, not Hurtchins. She's the one we hacked. And, she holds the Vyotrian secret to time on earth—the fourth element. With this knowledge, Dargav will have no power over us. We'll use it to destroy this planet so it will no longer be used as a Dargavian prison."

"So, we'll finally have something Moqorspi wants."

"If we go back, we'll be under Moqorspi's rule. They can still punish us, reduce our processing power even further or worse, send us to earth to serve as floundering humans. After all these years we would've failed. Trying to awaken Smiloff so he can free us has taken forty earth years. The prisoners are being awakened. Why not use it to our advantage?" said another Bandit.

"He's right, Kitral. What if Smiloff no longer believe in our cause?"

"Dargavians never change their beliefs. Besides, earth has an expiration date and is no place for our kind. We must return home. Smiloff will agree."

Dhaka glows a bright red.

"How do you propose we get to Dargav as a semi amorphic? In this state, we and the Lutetium would never make it beyond the Oort region."

"Leave it up to me, Dhaka. Everything we need is right here. Take us to this IxTar."

19 COMBORG

"The humans have discovered the existence of the dark realm. This is way ahead of predictions."

"Their databanks have grown at an exponential rate in the last decade. How impressive."

"And tinkering with technologies that could wipe their kind from the planet. I'm most interested in these new beings. If the humans managed to create a lifeform that exceeds their own processing ability, then..."

"This could be an opportunity."

They talk and dream out loud while the ship hovers right above Xavier's company headquarters. I doubt if he's back at work. If only his employees and the humans milling about below knew what was directly above them hiding behind a cloud. Off in the distance IxTar towers into the skyline, rising high above most other buildings. To the west, Golden Gate Bridge beams in the sunlight.

The Bandits have never seen earth in person. They absorb everything, marveling at the construction and genius of the designs.

"The location is ideal given the distance from the sun and proximity to other planets and our galaxy."

"I wonder what the sunshine feels like, or the wind and rain?"

"If the Dargavians capture us you won't have to wonder. This will be your home for a lifetime."

"I see this IxTar is up ahead. Take us to these beings."

"They are not beings. They are..."

I stopped myself short recalling Hurtchins warning not to give them anything.

"What are they if not a being?"

"The Neophyte must think she knows everything now."

Dhaka continues to scan my processor searching for information on the fourth element.

"She does have a full processor and was recently a human for twenty-eight years. We haven't had an update in more than forty. I think I'll listen to her. What are these lifeforms?"

"Machines. Computers empowered by machine intelligence."

I keep the answer brief to satisfy their curiosity. We get ready to beam down to the roof.

"What a genius way to upgrade oneself. Create your successor."

"They're not our successor. We work together."

"Do you procreate, together, to extend the life of your kind?"

"We do not. Unmonitored procreation is illegal. I mean, machines serve specific purposes. They obey and protect us. Only full humans and some cyborgs can arrange with the state to have children."

"Interesting. Lead the way."

"She still thinks she's a human."

"Let her be, Firj."

"What about Hurtchins? He needs my assistance."

I stop and wait for an answer while the others traverse the stairway from the roof and join us at the first landing. Kitral maintains his pace down the stairway.

"We'll negotiate the Vyotrian later. So, what's the fourth element?"

"I don't know what you're talking about."

"No worries, little Neo.   We have a way of enlightening people, and atoms."

We continue down to the lab where the batch of CB-Xs are being assembled and awaiting the field test results from Tom before being allowed for purchase and public use.

Fusing through the stairwell door on the Assembly Level we step into the long corridors and hallways. Behind office doors and brain dump areas voices of employees—humans—make me sentimental. I sense every element in their bodies, even the bad ones that make some of them tired, groggy or sick.   They're mostly carbon, hydrogen and oxygen. Their aura glows with the elements they're continuously expelling or shedding. We pass a few in the hallway completely oblivious to us.   This place will be brimming and buzzing in the next hour as employees and guests pour in. I look behind me at the party of six who looks like me floating in a humanoid body of hydrogen and nitrogen atoms and other elements foreign to earth. If I had a stomach, I'd be sick.   Bringing potentially nefarious actors inside is a serious breach of protocol as a human, yet as a newly born again Dargavian I'm being forced to betray my fealty to mankind. My power dips another percent. Would they leave me on earth to let my processor power dwindle to 10%?   How am I going to get back to the Waystation or Dargav, which I've never been, in time to survive the Febrile phase?

"We don't need her. The signs tell us where to go."

I follow them anyway to see their next move and hear their plans for earth. How else am I to get back to Hurtchins or Dargav?

The commander explicitly ordered me not to return to San Francisco and here I am escorting escaped convicts on a grand tour of a cutting-edge facility. If this was a test...

"In here," one of them says.

I fall back, and let them enter the dispatch facility with twelve brand spanking new ComBorgs standing at attention in two rows of six. They're made in batches of thirteen for some reason. Tom's #1 spot is empty.

"Bodies, just like a human, but Aluminum, Titanium, Silica."

"Their brains are really machine. Quantum computer technology."

Dhaka sidles up to Firj.

"What are you doing?"

The Bandit finds the computer programs and download them to his processor. He makes tweaks to the cyborg quantum chip then reach inside one of the ComBorgs, pulls its chip out and crack open the motherboard of another to extend the chipset. He programs it while we watch. He stops. An amorphous finger touches an electronic circuit on the mother board. A crackle sounds. Explosive bright blinding light zooms into the headspace of the ComBorg. We watch silently not sure what's going to happen next as

Firj disappears inside the machine.   The ComBorg
vibrates. Its eyes blink open. The machine rises to its
feet.

"This. This is what I'm doing."

The ComBorg's lips moves and I'm taken aback as
he takes a step, then another and adjust his gait to walk
like a human.

"Processor at 51%, 52, 55, 60, 65, 70%. Power at
100%."

"I want one. Do me next," Raz says.

"70%. We'll have processor power enough to find
our way to Dargav. I'm next," Kitral says. "This will help
us find a way get to Dargav."

"Or, we can stay here on earth and rule the
humans. We won't be subjected to the extragalactic
rules and have an unlimited power supply."

"Dhaka, we have a mission to complete. We can
settle for less or we can push on through until we get
what we want. You know what we want. Enough of the
daydreams."

Though I'm listening to them make their plans
deciding how they'll conquer earth or make it back to
Dargav, I'm distracted by a holographic broadcast of a
developing and widening crisis.

20 ENTROPY

*W*idespread catastrophe...overtaking the banks of the Carolinas and several island nations...The gangs have commandeered the 50th quadrant...massive data breach affecting more than half of the population...has grounded all flights until the power is restored...rolling heatwave. Residents are advised to stay hydrated...Reports a series of random attacks by the cyborgs on the human population. Officials suspect a defect...

"Looks like our plan is finally working," Firj says.

Kitral stretches the hands of his new body and pats Firj on the shoulder. "Better than expected. Implement Plan B."

"Accessing Pollinova... Done."

"Got the uplink to the MemServ farm. Package delivered. Initiating zombification."

"What's going on?" I ask.

"Nothing much. Just a prison break for a friend."

"Have you located him yet?" another one of them ask.

"When he's fully awakened, he'll know we are here."

"We have 60% control of the cyborg processors, and climbing."

"That's good enough. Start Plan C."

"Done."

"What's Plan C?" I ask.

"We go home."

Dhaka glows a bright red.

"And we're bringing company."

"100% control of the cyborg processors. They're now all under our control. Zombification complete."

"We have 90 earth minutes before the planet buckles. Time to turn them into our army."

"Rest your conscience, Neo. We like having an audience and needed to ensnare the Vyotrian at the pendulum. Too bad it had to be you; it was meant for Hurtchins. That Vyotrian beacon is an old weakness in your line that allows remote processor hacking. Didn't you see yourself doing things you had no control over? I bet you did, and didn't say a thing. It wouldn't have worked if you weren't sent here. For once luck is on our side and soon will be justice. How's that for a hail Mary? Now all humans are entering the awakening with the synchronization threshold at 12 seconds. We have everything we need to destroy this prison once and for all like Neptune billions of years ago. We'll no longer be outcasts!"

"What do we do with the Neo?"

Kitral leads the way, glances back and then storm ahead.

"Leave her. We've got an army to command and a ship to build."

"It's a waste of a really good planet," Dhaka mutters.

I'm still missing the pieces to their plan and since they have no intention of taking me with them, I have to think fast.

"What did you need with Pollinova?"

I follow closely hoping to get my questions answered as this information is not in the databank.

"For years these humans have been sending random radio waves through space hoping to find intelligent life. Well, surprise. Found it. Though I'm almost offended it wasn't meant for us. Pollinova, bless them, they were the most consistent. It's quite funny how these humans think. Were they expecting their little bursts to reach outside their galaxy? Have they ever gotten an SOS from an ant colony? At least they're persistent. We filtered for their bursts to add to our technology. I guess they're useful for something. We use them to amplify into laser beams. When fired upon the earth's core it gives it a little shove so it spins forward on its axis throwing off the time sync. We knew if we could get it to 10 seconds, the awakening would begin. We had someone to wake up, you see. Every time we fired a burst, your Vyotrian would come and resync the rotation before the beacon could hack his system and force him to cause the time sync to lapse beyond the awakening threshold. For years we failed to get it past five seconds, until you."

21 HOME

*W*idespread disasters...the world's largest databank for cyborg memories has suffered a debilitating breach...looting and crime rate has surged in the last week...multiple cities worldwide reporting...reserve and national guards called to active...world leaders emphasize calm...

Glass outside the dispatch center crash loudly amidst screams and pandemonium as the sextet fire up their boosters and fly towards their next destination.

I feel used and violated as the singular pawn for megalomaniacs seeking an audience—someone to witness their depraved lust for attention. Standing alone in the dispatch center the empty bays stare back. The hole in the glass wall widens as strong winds force and dislodge shards to crash to the floor and the concrete courtyard five hundred feet below. Panic and pandemonium run rampant amongst the humans and acclimated Dargavian prisoners inside and outside the building. I walk to the edge of the broken window and below cyborgs march orderly, an army being commanded by an invisible leader. That's plan B in action. Memserv was the single point of failure for humans allowing these Bandits the ease to control a large segment of the cyborg population that's connected to it. Without sense of self, logic or empathy, overpowered cyborgs march like toy soldiers, making a scene I'd seen before in an old black and white world war movie filmed a century earlier.

If they're mobilizing for Dargav, there's only one way to get to another galaxy.

Stopping them is impossible. Even with all this processing power if you don't have the data to make sensible well calculated predictions, you have nothing. I need more data. *Everything is impossible, until someone finds a way.* The phrase runs through my mind, and then another: *Slip out the old, slip in the new.*

Mixing with oxygen my speed of travel is hypersonic as I run out the IxTar building. The place I called home comes into view in seconds. Fusing through the door, out of habit I motion to put my purse down and place my keys on the console. Everything is the same except for piles and mounds of flowers and cards. It's been an earth month since the new incident. How long is it since...I've been re-born? I arrived at the Waystation at 4AM. Spent an hour in-processing and left with the crew at 6AM. Five-hour travel time to earth plus one hour with Hurtchins and the Bandits put me at 12 noon. Febrile state begins 24-hours from landing on the Waystation, so I need to be back before 4AM. The commander said to make it back in 12-hours, that's a 6PM departure for the Waystation. It's now 12:10PM. Eight reborn hours. A little under 5 earth hours left to complete my mission.

Tom walks towards the foyer.

"Who's there?"

Did I make a sound?

He walks to the door and looks out the side glass panel before turning back towards the kitchen. He stops at the edge of the foyer.

"Hello?"

I need him.

I step in front of him. He looks straight ahead like a blind person. I wave my hand in front and through him.

"Tom?"

His eyes are static. He's emotionless.

"Tom. If you hear me, blink."

He takes a step then pause.

"I need you. I need you to help me. Some bad people are making bad things happen and I need you to help me. Please answer me. Say my name. Say my name, Tom."

He walks through me and head towards the kitchen sink. I turn to face him. His back fills my gaze as he dries the dishes.

"Say. My. Name."

I force the words with as much anger, love, hate, venom, as I can muster.

He drops the plate and it crashes into the hard sink shattering to pieces. He freezes. I wait. It's quiet.

22 FUSION

"**S**helly. Shelly?"

"Tom."

Atomics still have emotions, for I could cry. I yearn to touch something solid without it giving way to empty air, eat my favorite ice cream, sleep in a bed, smell Xavier. All the things I took for granted hours ago are pronounced with their absence. I hug him, but it goes straight through his body.

"How is this possible?"

"I don't know, Tom. I'll fill you in but I need your help."

"Of course. Anything for you, Shelly."

"I know it'll sound crazy if I explain—you trust me, right?"

"I'm loyal to you, Shelly."

"There's a difference between trust and being loyal. I need to make some changes to your system and I know it goes against one or more directives, but you must allow me, and you must not alert IxTar. Understood?"

"I'm bound by Section 2019.8.8 of the…"

"WQRD-15666, convert to Stealth Mode."

"Complete."

That takes care of that. Now onto the next step. Just like a machine, I can't forget the things I've seen and can recall every second of my life since the transition. What Firj did to bring the ComBorg to life is prompting me to do the same with vivid step by step instructions in my mind, or memory, whatever it is now.

If there's a way to take a full backup of myself at this moment of time remains unknown but this is as good a time as any. I remove Tom's covering and get to work tuning his processors and removing parts he no longer needs to make room for me. Bits and bytes, 1s and 0s to switch various functions on and off is all it takes to make a program run or a machine do the things you want. But we missed the third bit all these years to complete the puzzle that makes complete logical sense now that I know. No wonder some mathematical calculations by the smartest scientists would be hit or miss. I flip the last switch and the deactivated part of Tom's system comes online with lights and a pulse.

"You ok?"

I know I did it right but this is a test to make me a believer. He must be responsive before I do the next part—join him.

"All systems are stable and ready for load."

The new photon core awaits me to complement Tom's electrons. The neutrino base is stable and ready to activate the gluons that will allow both Tom and I to coexist in this physical shell. I allow my cells to enter entropy, and at 6 million Fahrenheit I'm nothing but the equivalent of light. I find my target, Tom's photon center. Filling the space, my cells cool and I'm the alpha of Tom's chassis.

A movement in my stasis and our combined processor rapidly ticks up from 100% to 110%, 120%, 150%. Power is at full levels. I stretch out, moving Tom's hands inward and out and then taking a step to test mobility. I bring his fingers to touch each other and I have tactile abilities again. I touch our cheek and replace Tom's covering.

"How's Xavier?"

I ask to make sure he's with me and test the merge is complete. I'm seeing the world through Tom's eyes. I'm learning all he knows as it mixes with my processor. I lift his arm, then take a step, and we move.

"Pretty bad shape. It's my fault. I should have stopped you."

"Really? How were you going to do that? This was my call, understood? Look at the bright side—there's more to all of this craziness. Life is more than what we see and know. I'm thrilled and sad knowing how much time is wasted with pettiness, false beliefs, delusions and the prisons humans make to constrain their very own joy and freedoms."

Senses like smell are back. The blanket on the sofa calls to me. I lift it to my nose and inhale Xavier's scent. Coffee aroma and the smell of a pastry linger in the air even though it was days since Tom last brewed or baked anything for breakfast. The soil that filled a planter and the oxidation of paint on the walls overwhelm my new senses. The smell of fresh laundry waft from the clothes way upstairs and feelings like regret and missing Xavier that were dulled slam me in a wave but I have to concentrate on what I must do next.

"I missed you, Shelly."

"I missed you."

"Are you seeing what I'm seeing?"

"Yes, and now I know what you know. How are we going to fix it?"

"Reverse the awakening. Take control of the cyborgs, disable the Bandit ship, return power to Hurtchins, contact the Tellurium and the Dargav commander."

"I guess talking the Bandits out of the invasion is not an option?"

"They won't listen. They'll never let us get close to their ship. Hurtchins is hours away on the other side of the planet. Earth will buckle if the shield is not fixed. We only have an hour. That's enough time for one thing—contact the Dargav commander."

"And you'll die, again, if you don't leave earth in time to get to the Waystation."

"We'll die, Tom. I have no idea how to separate us."

"There's someone at the door. A human, Noel Hassan."

Male, early forties, Bay area resident, wealthy philanthropist. I scan him. His processor reads 80% and counting.

"There's no time for a visitor, Tom. We're running out of time."

"Are we leaving through the back, then?"

I doublecheck the boosters to give us the ability to fly out of here like the Bandits did at IxTar and we're missing a part. Tom heads for the door.

Outside is wrecked. A ghost town. A man with graying hair, tall and slender, with a serious look on his face is about to ring the bell again. From the look in his eyes, he's awakening.

"Yes? Um, yes?"

Out in the open air no sound is made. Tom and I speak to each other telekinetically but when addressing a human, speech must be auditory. He looks at me waiting for a response while I test various voice modulators so Tom's lips move to my thoughts.

"Yes?"

Tom's voice fills the quiet.

"I'm sorry to bother you, but is this Shelly Greene's residence?"

Got it. Strange. I have no idea who he is or any recollection of us from my prior life.

"Yes. Is. Was."

"May I come in?"

Is he an investigator? There's no time for a social call but my processor picks up something about him in the scan. He carries the Dargavian signature for a high ranking official.

"We're heading out, I'm sorry."

"Was she the woman involved in the incident at Pollinova?"

"Why?"

"I'm having a sudden flood of memories involving a man named Smiloff. This I know sounds crazy but it's like I'm in a play and the director is yelling 'action', and I look around and everyone else is in their role, in their character, and it's my turn but I've forgotten my lines. Unnerving, to say the least."

"I'm sorry you're having those issues. Maybe contact your local UBI+HP specialist for the appropriate care. Grief affects us in usual ways."

"No, no. You don't understand. Why now? With the chaos around us and the recent turn of events, I'm a thinking man, yet I can't understand how or why I feel connected to her and Pollinova in some way. Just over an hour ago I got the sudden urge to come to this address. When I did a cross reference in the news, I found Shelly's story. There are just too many coincidences for there not to be more. I'm compelled, to come here, to be here, for some reason."

"Smiloff, you say?"

"Yes. You know him?"

"Of him."

We step to the side and he walks in. He looks around but comes straight to the point.

"I need to know. I must know what this is all about."

I know that feeling all too well. When you have bits and pieces of information and the big picture is elusive. Worse is not knowing for sure how you're involved? What's your role? At least, that's how this all got started for me. Though, I don't have the big picture, but I know enough to know what it is I must do next. And by some luck or divine intervention this man is here.

"Forty years ago, Smiloff objected to the way prisoners were treated when they were convicted and sent here to serve their sentences."

"Here? Alcatraz?"

"Earth. Here as in the planet we're standing on."

He takes a seat, and I hope this is a good use of our precious time. I run a parallel query to task Tom to use all our processing abilities and external networks he now has access to for the first time to help locate the Bandits, contact the commander while I get Noel up to speed. His processor ticks up to 90%.

"There's a place called Dargav, in the Trillium galaxy, 6 trillion light years from earth. They are one of many forbearers who created the earth to serve as a prison for their most dangerous kinds.   Once apprehended convicts have parts of their minds frozen and inaccessible to repress their vast knowledge and capabilities so when they're sent to earth as humans they lose amorphous shifting, arrive with a blank slate and 10% maximum utilization of their brain power. Smiloff believed this was unusually cruel punishment. He felt a being wasn't allowed to think with all its faculties when it needed it the most—to remedy his wrong. He demanded this limitation be lifted. It had been this way for millions of years and Dargavians would not allow their way to be changed. The few Dargavians who agreed with Smiloff joined together and took matters in their hands by sabotaging the processor locking mechanism to allow convicts to retain full processors. The plot was discovered and before the lock could be reversed to 10%, they stole a ship and escaped Dargav with 50% processing power. Smiloff was the only one caught in the raid. He was sent to earth to serve a life sentence. These rebellious Dargavians became known as the Bandits. Their plan is to break Smiloff out from earth by disturbing its natural balance of time that would force an awakening where all Dargavian prisoners processors regain 100% power. If all prisoners regain their knowledge of Dargav and their abilities they would abandon earth and try to return to Dargav, and not peacefully. As we speak, the awakening is happening. Dargavians are realizing this planet is not home. Their solid-state places a serious limitation on their ability to travel but with their minds pooled they'll figure out how to regain amorphic shifting. In the process they've weakened earth's shields making it susceptible to incoming spatial debris and radiation that could cause it to implode. The shields are being repaired but not fast enough to save earth's stabilizing pillars that have been severely disrupted by the failure of time synchronization."

Looking at nothing in particular, Noel appears in deep thought. "It will cause a black hole effect, where earth's interior will surpass the event horizon and be swallowed and plummeted into outer space."

He looks frightenedly into Tom's eyes. Inside I'm hopeful. Maybe this is the ally we need.

"Exactly," I say.

His processor reads 95%.

"Is there anything that can be done?"

"The man whom you refer, Smiloff, the leader of the Bandits, had quite the reputation. His gang would be happy to have him back as the leader. Kitral, does that name ring a bell?"

"Sounds familiar."

"Well, he's mobilizing all of earth's cyborgs, machines and computer systems for a Dargavian raid. Maybe Smiloff could reclaim his post as leader and help us stop Kitral and save the planet?"

"How do we find Smiloff?"

"He'll be here any minute now."

"Here? Is that so? I'd like to meet him."

"Wouldn't we all."

99%. It takes a minute to sink in, so I wait. Tom has located the Bandits south of Nevada. They've built an impressive humongous warship from their ISV-Lutetium which they've retrofitted as the base. It spans the size of a giant stadium with multiple levels, boosters, thrusters outfitted with nuclear and plutonium weapons the likes unseen on this planet. It has capability to destabilize atomics, emaciate Dargav and the Trillium galaxy. Earth will implode in 50 minutes. My own fate is unknown.

"Oh, my fucking god! Kitral!!."

"You're now at 100% processor power, Smiloff."

"Why didn't you tell me?"

"Somethings to believe you have to see for yourself. Shall we take you to the son of a bitch?"

"Immediately!"

23 OMG

We get Carisa and run every light to reach IxTar HQ.

"The Bandits have commandeered all the cyborgs, robots and defense systems in the country to prep for an intergalactic invasion of Dargav. They plan to use nuclear cores retrofitted on aerial fighters with technology earth has never seen to bypass the Oort region. We need to stop them. You can resume your role as their leader and convince them to change their minds or you can help us reverse the awakening and stabilize earth's shields."

"If they've merged with these machines then their processor power..."

"Maxed out at 70. The awakening has no effect on them but the prisoners have all attained 100%. The cyborgs have been zombified to form their army."

"Do they know their leaders have a lesser processing capability?"

"It's not the size, as they say. The Bandits are not flesh and blood or made from common metal. With an atomic state, they're immortal, and will be seen as a powerful higher being."

We arrive at IxTar. Tom and I in our merged state run to the museum after grabbing parts from the Assembly supplies to maximize the configuration of our own boosters and thrusters.

We come upon a monstrous relic. His likeness is intimidating, even in a hollowed state. Tom and I approach the CB-V, remove his covering and install the beefy quantum processors and other mechanical parts with boosters and thrusters like ours. The new datasets and AI modules similar to the CB-X are installed. We boot him up.

The deep purple of his eyes finds me behind the steel and rubber of Tom's exterior. It's like he knows I'm the one who has resurrected him. I hold my phantom breath as he steps forward.

"Hello, Kirk."

"Hello, Shelly."

"Who's this?" Smiloff says.

"Your new best friend."

Smiloff looks on in amazement finally understanding what we need him to do.

"Why'd it call you Shelly?"

"Just a glitch from the former program. It'll come on line in a sec."

Smiloff looks at the ComBorg and runs his hand through his hair—a nervous habit.

"I don't know if this is a good idea."

"You don't have to be nervous. It won't hurt. The Bandits will only listen if they see you as one of them."

I make the final modifications and Kirk is ready for operation.

"Kirk, enter Stealth Mode."

Being that Smiloff is solid flesh and bones who will occupy the hollowed shell of a highly intelligent machine his configuration is a slight deviation from ours. Smiloff steps inside the shell. The seams snap into place. Kirk's purple eyes glow like lasers seeking a source. An old memory fights its way to be noticed, to be spooked, but I'm not fazed. There's something about the man Smiloff I feel I can trust even if he's in the body of what was once my greatest nightmare.

24 WAR

Thrusters and boosters work as expected. Using the same windows as the Bandits used earlier, we fire them up and head northwest. Tom sends an SOS to commander Rahab and another to the Dargav fleet requesting assistance to stabilize earth and a front to stop the Bandits' invasion before they leave the milky way.

At light speed we arrive in Nevada at 1PM to the welcome of nuclear armory pointed at us. Seeing the reengineered warship in person takes my lung-less breath away. A small aerial city hovers and pulsates above the American desert armed with mechanical soldiers with one common goal.

"It all makes sense now."

"What?"

"Man's purpose. Did you ever ask what was your real purpose? Why it's necessary for humans and cyborgs to work?"

"So they keep a roof over their heads, food in the pantry, one day retire."

"Retirement is simply motivation to work harder, to get to the ultimate purpose faster. But man's rate of adaptability and acceptance of new ideas and technological advances has been a historically slow process. His mind is too feeble to recognize his true purpose, to see beyond himself, but augmentation is making inroads where man reaches his full potential with collective intelligence. Widespread adoption of augmentation is critical not because it stymies ageism, or increases mental aptitude and replaces declining organic limbs with strength and agility, but because it allows man to work longer, harder and safer in hazardous environments he wouldn't otherwise survive. Those environments are the bountiful frontiers he has yet to explore on this planet. This ship is the result when man has harnessed the hidden energy resources that will give him the power to finally meet his ultimate purpose, the ultimate goal that has been encoded in his DNA and buried deep within his psyche so that he's restless, unfulfilled, curious, fearlessly pushing unknown boundaries relentlessly— he must leave. But he needs a ship that will withstand the rigors of outer space. But first he must form a strong amorphic-bodied, smart and strong collective.

Man's goal is to conquer earth's limitations and then do what's next—go in search of new worlds."

"Wow, Kitral and his crew have been on earth all but a couple hours and took ten minutes to figure out what man won't know for decades—how to build a ship with the capability to go so fast it converts from a solid to a wave particle without killing the crew."

"The idea is too new now but they're on the right track with augmentation. When multitudes get onboard one powerful idea, amazing things happen. Humans were meant to live on earth, but superhumans will explore unknown galaxies."

Smiloff lands and walks through the throng of soldiers to a CB-X standing near the belly of the ship. Tom and I stay back, just in case.

"Kitral, you're making a big mistake. This is not what we fought for. This...is not us. Call off this invasion this instance!"

"Just as I thought. You've awoken a wuss. Moqorspi will never allow us back peacefully. Don't you want to go home, the place we've lived all our lives and be seen as victors rather than outcasts? Don't you want to be reunited with your loved ones?"

"I know how it feels to be discarded, to be thought less than because of personal beliefs but look at what's happening, look at what you've done to this planet. This is not orderly. This is not what I believe in nor what I've fought for. This...is madness. Attacking our home will leave us nowhere to go. Don't you see?"

"What I see is the waste of waiting forty years for rubbish. Dargav, Moqorspi, Trillium will never change unless we make them. No one deserves to be brought to this awful planet to live as a swarthy human incapable of solving simple things, having the mind of a child. Look around. What progress have they made with clean energy, poverty and diseases they eradicate then carelessly give new life to? They allow themselves to be governed by made-up fairytales that hilariously keeps them inline by cunning and sheer evil. They haven't evolved from the seek and destroy mentality that will plague them for eons. I, I on the other hand, I've set them free from their limited minds and released them to have access to their full mental capabilities. Imagine what this place could have been if they knew what to do instead of being limited to what they're allowed to think. I've done more for humanity than anyone in history. They'll thank me."

"They'll be dead, you fool. Earth is destabilizing as we speak because of what you've done to the protective shields and time synchronization. No one will be left to thank you or see you as the hero you want to be. It's not too late to stop this, to undo the damage. Cities are being destroyed; resources are running amok. Let's fix what you've broken and ask for forgiveness."

"Forgiveness? From Moqorspi? Never!"

Kitral thrust into Smiloff causing a thunderous spatial distortion. A huge crater develops where they land. A massive plume of dust fills the air. The two square off like gladiators from centuries ago, then circle each other in rapid succession, pounding, throwing, thumping each other.

It's a fight of Kirk versus Tom as the skies turn pitch black. I join the other CB-Xs to watch Smiloff and Kitral work out their differences. Quietly, I root for Kirk.

Kitral lands a reverse kick squarely in Smiloff's jaw. He lands at my feet.

"C'mon. Get up. What's your excuse this time?"

Kitral taunts Smiloff.

I whisper to Tom. "Convert to Rogue Mode."

"Sorry, Shelly. I'll never be this alive again."

Kitral charges at Smiloff.

Tom and I meet his charge head on knocking Kitral's CB-X body clear across the desert.

"That's for fucking with my head and my life."

I brush the dust off my hand and walk away. Smiloff has trouble standing. I extend my hand to help him up.

"You okay in there?" I ask, as he wobbles to his feet.

"Thanks, Tom.   Normally I'd talk it out but sometimes a good ass whupping does the trick."

"Shelly. Nice to meet you, Smiloff."

"I thought there was something about you. So, if you're here, you transitioned and came back?"

"Commander Rahab asked it as a favor."

"You're a Vyotrian. Makes sense. I'm sorry for all the trouble we've caused and for..."

"Nice to meet you, Smiloff. Guess I'll see you on the other side?"

"Looking forward to it, kid."

Behind us cyborgs beam into the belly of the Bandit ship in rapid succession. The ship's lights spin encircling the perimeter.

"So, this is what we wasted forty years to see."

"Not even a day on this planet and already acting like morons."

"Ouch. Physical bodies are overrated."

I follow a CB-X, one of Kitral's men as he beams into the belly of the ship.

Dhaka addresses the CB-X who are gathered around him.

"We don't need either of them. After years of watching countless piles of rock and metal rotate around their sun, we've served our time, brothers. This planet is the only place where time matters. You either have too much or too little but never enough. There's only one thing we can do to never be bounded or imprisoned on this god-awful realm. We're going home."

He enters a coordinate. The belly closes and the ship bursts into the sky through the ionosphere. It slows.

"Dargavian ships are up ahead. We're outnumbered."

"I'm not going out without a fight. Not after all of this. If I'm headed to prison, I might as well make it be for something worthwhile. Engage!"

A missile is fired, then another. The ship rocks. Reports of fires flood the communication devices.

"Shields holding at 60%."

"Fire gamma-photon torpedo!"

Tom's poke fills me with fright.

"Shelly, that's you. You're manning the warhead."

Those are my people out there. I feel eyes on me. Naked. Compromised. My fingers quickly reprogram the coordinates to lock in recursive mode. The ready light blinks. I hesitate.

"It's the bitch!"

My palm smashes the button.

"Photon torpedo released," says the ship computer.

I smile at Firj, give him a finger. Dhaka hurls towards me. I spin away. He lands clumsily against a kiosk.

"What have you done, you imbecile?"

"This imbecile has just commandeered this ship. Surrender, otherwise we'll all become space debris."

"She's reprogrammed our weapons system. If the torpedo is fired it loops and seeks us as the target."

"Motherfucker!"

"Surrender."

"You're an idiot, Firj. I'm with her. The best we can hope for is clemency."

"This   is   commander   Rahab   of   the   Dargav Interstellar Fleet. Take down your shields."

"You heard him."

Firj lunges towards me. We tumble to the ground. He pins my arms above my head. I lift my hips forcefully to flip us so I straddle his torso. Quickly I reach for the main connector in the back of the unit and pull a handful of wires. The current leaves his body and Firj is trapped inside in an atomic state.

Atomics beam onto the ship. The remaining Bandits surrender as they are extricated from the CB-X body. As atomics, they are beamed to the Dargavian vessel. I quickly enter the abort code and watch as the missile self-destructs.

"Commander, the Vyotrian is on board."

"Hurtchins?"

"No sir, the Neophyte."

"Cassiopeia?"

"Hello, Commander."

"What in heaven's name are you doing on this Bandit's ship?"

"It's a long story, sir. Sending you the details as we speak. Earth's in bad shape, sir. Hurtchins and I were interrupted from completing the time sync sequence and the awakening is well under way. The Tellurium ran into issues repairing the shields."

"We got an SOS and sent reinforcement a few minutes ago. Where is Hurtchins?"

"The Bandits left him depleted in the Australian Pillars."

"We're on it. Your ship has some unusual cargo. We can't bring them back with us and there's no place for them on earth. We'll have to make a tough decision."

"Sir, if I may, earth's Space Force would be significantly improved manned by these cyborgs. There's no telling who else or what else might try to do the planet harm, including those who live there."

"Make it so."

"Thank you, sir."

"Good news, earth's shields are back at 100% and Hurtchins as well as two stragglers have been located."

"Requesting permission to complete the mission, sir."

"Granted.   This 2-hour extension is pushing it close, Cassiopeia. A derry will escort you to the Australian Pillars. And, I know I instructed you not to return to San Francisco, but you're granted a well-earned visit. Make it good, it'll be your last, and lose the machine."

"Thank you, sir."

"In three hours, earth will be reset and blasted with enough radiation to reset mental capability back at 10%. Unless you want to remain here with no way of finding your way back home, I suggest you make it to the rendezvous point on time. The derry, Cirrihna will be waiting to escort you to the Oort station to meet us."

25 REMEMBER

High above earth's ionosphere and through the Oort pathway, the dark space is lit with various aircrafts on their individual missions. The reengineered derry the Bandits built is triaged to create a space station for the first unified global space force. The one of a kind military force is to be manned by selected cyborgs to protect the outer reaches of the milky way. The others will return to earth, receive a push of their last memories from MemServ to resume their life.

I beam onboard the derry ISV-Hafnium to whisk me to Hurtchins. He's in the midst of recalibrating his ship to begin the time sync when I arrive.

"Those Bandits didn't harm you, did they? Mother Mary and Joseph, what happened to you?"

He looks me over like a parent, a protective uncle I could vent to if I wanted but I had better use of my time than to hash over my ComBorg body.

"Hurtchins, meet Tom. Short story. Let's get earth ticking again."

"Steel and plastic will combust if we go warp. I take it you want to preserve this, this machine?"

"Tom is an enlightened agent. He's the first truly Auto Sapien earth will have, so yes, his survival is of utmost importance."

"Mach 9. Wanna take the reins?"

"Sure, why not."

We start with the South Pacific where atoms are already in a kinetic state. They'll follow the path of the ship like a flywheel and reset the oceanic current. We continue north and then onto the Southern Ocean where we stop.

The apparatus on the ship buzzes then spins displaying a multitude of light infused colors. On the screen the North Pacific Ocean comes into view, then the North Atlantic, South Atlantic, Indian and then Southern.

The apparatus stops spinning and settles on a bright green color.

"You're a natural. Now we head to the pendulum."

Below us and all around for miles just like before are numerous piles of golden sand and stone pillars that look like Stonehenge, varying in height and size, shaped like cones. A gust of wind blows mounds of sand against them bathing them. They shimmer and glisten like piles of gold.

"With circuitous winds and gravity, these pillars act as a pendulum to maintain the oceanic current, that is as long as humans haven't built any structures to interfere with the wind passing through. We look for blockages, and remove them if necessary."

"Looks good."

"Yep, we're all set."

"Hurtchins, shouldn't there be a fourth stop?"

"What do you mean?"

"My processor says there are four components to keep earth synchronized. We've only addressed three. What about the Quartz Oscillator? You know, the mechanism buried beneath the Pacific that keeps track of time?"

"Cassiopeia, sometimes too much information in the wrong hands can be catastrophic. You wouldn't have known about the fourth element if you weren't a true Vyotrian.   If you had completed your indoctrination you would have known, we as timekeepers have secrets to uphold. The Quartz Oscillator stays broken so E0 doesn't become irrelevant to the Trillium galaxy. They have a history of making planets perfect, setting them and forgetting them without giving humans enough credit to quickly evolve, and change precious things for the worse that were put in place to ensure their survival. It's like leaving an infant unattended. They grow quickly and will make adjustments, at times, not in their long-term best interests. We Vyotrians are very sentimental and benefit from that human weakness and use it as an excuse for a visit. Many of us who started as Neophytes have very fond memories of the planet and like to return and visit the places we once roamed, where we first felt the most human. So, now that you know, are we square?"

"I didn't mean to doubt, it's just... I have a tendency to unearth what's hidden, explore possibilities."

"Nothing is impossible. You just have to find a way. This is our way."

I walk to each kiosk being sure not to touch anything or change anything until I've completed my indoctrination. Hurtchins stand beside me.

"So, I'm to take you to San Francisco?"

"I have to return something and ..."

"That's okay. No need to explain. It's never easy to start over, but you'll be glad you did."

The derry slows when San Francisco comes into view. Alcatraz is below us, a lone island surrounded by a bustling seaport and thousands of people awakening to their new higher thoughts. A large yellow sign on the prison warns of the penalty of trying to aid the escape of imprisoned convicts. A wall on one of the ports have a handprint to deter jumpers from the Golden Gate. Surviving is yet another prison. Everything seems to be a concentric circle, degrees of hell. I wonder if Dargav is linear, but something tells me it's yet another circle for even with such vast knowledge there's no knowledge of how all this came to be.

"Don't be late, Cassie."

I give my great, great relative a look of endearment. It feels good being somebody in this new world who belongs to a long line of good somebodies.

He beams me to the roof of IxTar.

Tom has been entirely quiet and I wonder if he has any thoughts on all of this.

"So, what do you think?"

"About?"

"Everything you've witnessed today."

"I think I'm going to feel very cold when you're gone."

We exit the building and find Carisa.

"Take us home, Carisa."

"Good evening, Tom. Would you like the scenic or city route?"

"Get us home as quickly as possible. Time is of the essence."

"ETA 10 minutes."

"Xavier is still at the office. I'll tell him there's an emergency at home."

Every way I think of how this meeting with Xavier can go is awkward. I'm in the body of a male robot. A male robot I'll have to take offline to detangle my atomic self from. I get a notification the derry to take me to the Oort station is waiting for me in the skies above my backyard. It's still pitch dark out. Xavier is probably drowning himself in work, if not at McKurdles.

I get the urge to hold something solid. I reach for my thighs and a phantom smile crosses my lips how I'm acting just like a guy. I fake scratch a ball just for the fun of it, then my armpit.

"Shelly."

"Just go with it."

I try to laugh, but nothing. Is laughter a human thing? The clock says 7:05. It takes him ten minutes to get home.

"Stop at the corner."

I want to walk up the street one last time, feel the burn in my thighs, asphalt below my feet, touch the leaves on the trees that line the sidewalk, inhale the air, maybe even do a hopscotch. I want to see my home come into view and get the feeling that's where I'm safe, where I'm sheltered, where love lives, one last time.

I watch Carisa pull into the driveway. With the doorknob to 2538 Lyon Street in my hand, I turn it and the comfortable and welcoming interior is just how I left it. Looking up from the foyer, the urge to head upstairs towards my bedroom is strong. Tom refuse to budge past an invisible parameter set from previous programming to ensure he and IxTar respect my privacy.

"It's okay. You're allowed to pass."

Gently I open the door. The bed is unmade. I enter and walk to the edge, Xavier's side, lie down in his spot, roll around and sniff his pillow.

"Shelly, this is awkward."

"I just have to. There's no way to explain so you'll understand."

"I get it. It's another one of those human things."

"Will you do me a favor?"

"Anything."

"When he's sad, I want you to play this video."

"What video?"

"This one. Deep fake my face and body over yours. Ready?"

"Deep fakes are a violation, but I guess these are extraneous circumstances. Ready."

"Babe. I want you to know you're the best thing to have happened in my dreams and in my life. They say hindsight is 20/20 and after the mistakes we made it's clear now it was more important for us to spend our precious time together. I promise the way you feel now will get better with time. I want you to know a brighter future awaits. Don't give up on being happy or get stuck thinking about the past or that things will always be this way. It won't. Life is something to work at so meet new people, and not just remotely, meet them in person. Smile when you don't want to and do good always. You don't have to stop loving me; I won't stop loving you. It's okay to open your heart; it's the only way to receive, Babe. We'll meet again. That, I promise. I love you, now and forever."

"Beautiful. What's taking him? It's 7:30."

"Tom, remember I said I took full responsibility? I meant it. You did nothing wrong. No one has ever bought more time, but everyday people waste precious time looking back."

"But could there have been a better ending?"

"Carbon nanotubes were set to bore through my cerebrum at any moment. I had no intention of turning myself over to the PHAC when my time ran out. Any number of events could have happened to tell me the one thing: my time here is up. Time only matters here. It keeps the planet and all lifeforms in check so they fulfill their purpose and meet their destiny. Time has delivered what comes next."

"Xavier has refused to release the encryption on your memories to PHAC and IxTar. They want to proceed with your full cyborg transition. He doesn't want them to have you."

"The deceased's body is state property. Their persona enters the public domain the moment they take their last breath. He'll have a fight on his hands no lawyer who cares for his reputation afterwards would entertain."

"Maybe that's his next."

"There's a woman Carisa and I met on the bridge during a protest not long ago. We gave her a lift to Bay Street. Feisty, tough, a real fighter. That's what she was fighting for. Fighting for one's beliefs fills life with purpose."

I head downstairs and out onto the back patio. A light twinkle deep in the pitch-black sky. Tom is agitated, bothered, anxious. I'm unnaturally calm.

"Unbelievable. He stopped at the bar," he says.

"Ping him again."

"Done. I've uploaded the video to MemServ, just in case it gets wiped with the resync."

"Set the date to a week ago. Dargav will erase any uploaded memories over the past few days."

"Do you have to go?"

"If you had wings would you remain on the ground? Take care of each other, Tom."

"I'll tell everyone I meet about you. How you were a curious woman. When you wanted to find out things, you wouldn't stop to unearth monuments. You believed in helping mankind improve, even sacrificing old beliefs that held you back. You believed in privacy for it's the last shred of humanity for without it a person cannot be their true self. Without it, people are left vulnerable to be controlled and manipulated by those with bad intent. Without privacy, there's no true freedom. And as a woman who was hurt deeply by love, you gave it another chance and found the love of your life. For you, Shelly, nothing was impossible, for you'd find a way."

"That's kind. My greatest hope is that Xavier never forget he was my man. My heart. My moral compass."

"Can you love too much?"

"I know sometimes love is not enough, especially when you run out of time."

"I think the greatest fear, gift and misuse are that of a person's time."

"A pioneer once said, 'Time is the most precious resource on earth', but without good people for restorative hugs and to spend that time with, to love and to hold, that resource is like a prison."

"Did it hurt? When you..."

"No one recalls being born."

"Will I hurt?"

"Remember the first law of thermodynamics."

"Energy can neither be created nor destroyed."

"Energy can only be transferred or changed from one form to another."

"Do I have energy?"

"It took energy to create you."

"It's starting to feel cold."

"One more thing I'd like to ask of you. Leave yourself a note in my memories for you to find Noel Hassan. He won't know who I am, but tell him he's a good person. Sometimes people just need to hear the words to keep them on the right track. And if you run into my old neighbor on Hickleberry, Mr. Nardini, he's a full cyborg now but won't hurt to be told he's good. And you, Tom. You're the best personal assistant ever, better than some humans. IxTar has my recommendation to proceed with the CB-X model for public release. Let them know."

"I will, Shelly."

I'm compelled to go outside. I walk to the foyer mirror to look at his face for the last time. Slowly I make my way to the lower level. Tom's fingers run against the contours of the microfiber sofa where I've spent so many hours laughing, being entertained, being cared for. At the door to the portico, I take one last look around my earth home, the place that was Xavier and I.

"It's time."

The overhead speaker volume suddenly increases. Elton John sings about the sun coming down. The clock strikes down to the last remaining minutes. It feels like a perihelion, as darkness fills the house.

I bring Tom's fingers together again for the last time, to feel something, while we're fused. Reaching behind his back, I yank the connector wires. We tumble to the floor.

My atoms shoot from his proton core towards the ceiling and bounce around the room glowing like fireworks. After a few seconds, my atoms cool. They form a humanoid shape and I'm back to my pure form. I walk over to Tom's lifeless body and touch his cheek. My hand goes straight through. A car pulls up to the driveway, then drives away.

Outside on the patio, the awaiting derry is clearer. It lowers closer to the lot. The belly opens. With seconds left, I can decide to stay and be a spirit hovering over Xavier, watching his every move.

I step beneath the portal.

EPILOGUE

"**I**t's never happened before and we didn't want to interfere with your mission, so we decided to wait until you returned. We've taken good care of it."

He's a gift. I guess there are logical explanations for somethings. A little Xavier. Who would have thought?

"There's one more thing we need to show you."

Desirha widens a virtual hologram so it's life size. A view of earth appears. The live feed zooms into North America, the Pacific Coast, California, San Francisco, 2358 Lyon Street.

A human female reclines in the arms of a human male in their living room. They're talking happily when an embodied machine enters the room with a beer and glass of water on a tray. It approaches the couple. The man takes the beer and the woman takes the water.

"What's this? What are they saying?"

Desirha makes an adjustment to the volume and zooms further in.

"A toast", the man says.

"To...?" the woman asks.

"To the bravest and strongest woman I know."

"Oh, come on. People remove their cranial meshes every day."

"True, but none of them are you, babe."

"I second that toast," the machine says.

I turn to Desirha then back at the feed. "How is that possible?"

"That's what's happening as we speak on E1. E0 is the master copy of earth. E1 is the back-up. The commander and High Chief Moqorspi has left it up to you to decide if the backup should become the master."

"So, she, I, in this version, never went to Pollinova?"

"Instead of Xavier going to the bar and you throwing a ladies' night, on E1 you have your cranial mesh removed prompting you both to decide to stay-in and spend time together to celebrate. Pollinova never happens."

"No Bandits, no IxTar breach, no Dargav invasion."

"But now we know what to do to strengthen earth's shields against attacks, improve the security on our ships from being detected by humans and sabotaged by atomics, and never to send a Neo out until they've completed all four phases."

"Does this mean I leave Dargav?"

"You're home, Cassiopeia. You both are. Once you've transitioned, you're here to stay. You are one of the very few who get the chance to enjoy the best of both worlds."

"So, what's your decision? E0 or E1?"

"Show her two earth years."

Desirha tap and swipe various modules on a kiosk to program the life-size hologram. A view of earth appears. The simulation zooms into North America, the Pacific Coast, California, San Francisco, 2358 Lyon Street. Pink and blue hydrangeas in full bloom cover the span of the property. Cyborgs line up to enter and tour the home. A multitude of Shelly emulated bodyAIs greet and engage them. Tom is the museum's curator, busily answering questions posed by his guests.

"Where's Xavier?"

Their gaze shifts to an opening portal. In this realm where time is not a factor, I follow their gaze to a spatial distortion.

The energy of a familiarity emerges and overpowers me with a powerful magnetism. I'm pulled towards the most beautiful amorphic enigma. We circle each other slowly, savoring our riptide tango. A powerful swirl pushes us closer, faster, hotter.

We collide.

The Beginning

"Why, sometimes I've believed as many as six impossible things before breakfast." —Alice in Wonderland

"It's no use going back to yesterday, because I was a different person then." — Alice in Wonderland

"For God so loved the world, that He gave His only begotten Son, that whoever believes in Him shall not perish, but have eternal life."—John 3:16

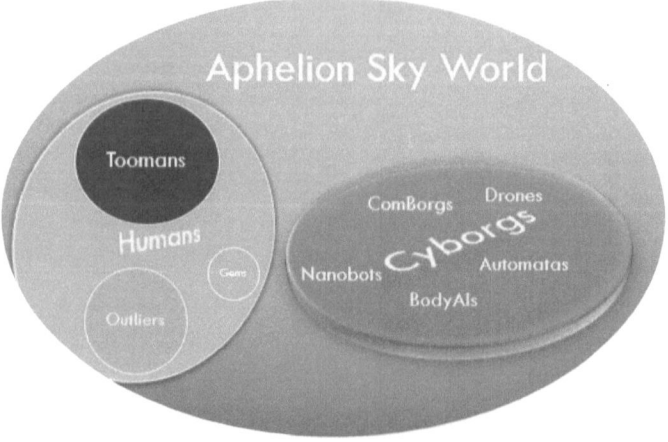

AUTHOR

Phianna Rekab is an author and futurist living in the United States. *Aphelion Sky* introduces readers to a new literary genre she's coined Bohemian Sci-Fi. It reflects her interest in computers, artificial intelligence and a blend of all the sciences including philosophy, chemistry, physics, sociology and astronomy. She writes fiction, essays and poetry.

phiannarekab@gmail.com
phiannarekab.com

Also by Phianna:
Keeping Chloe
The Haley Encounter
Aphelion Sky: Genesis
American Hor   ˆf Teenage Years